I0741894

Unearthly Fables

DAVID SCHEMBRI

Unearthly Fables.

Schembri, David.
Unearthly Fables / David Schembri.
Edited by Paula Berinstein

Layout, graphic design, and illustrations by David Schembri.

Acknowledgements:
David Conyers, Kirstyn McDermott, Amanda J Spedding, Martin Livings, Andrew J McKiernan, Rhonda Schembri, Chuck McKenzie, Marty Young, Jason Nahrung, Kaaron Warren, Juliet Bathory, Kyla Lee Ward, Robert Hood, Lee Battersby, Mark Farrugia, Greg Chapman, Brett McBean, Shane Jiraiya Cummings, Cameron Trost, and *Matthew Tait.*
Thank you for your wonderful contributions!

Special thanks to:
Rhonda, Anthony, and Eve. Paula and Alan. Mum and Dad. My entire family for their support.
Marty, Amanda, Jules and Mark. Claire and Leon for encouraging me to pursue this idea,
Charles Danny Lovecraft, Daniel Watson, Tracy Sauso-Bawa, Geoff Brown, and the AHWA.

www.writingshow.com
http://davidschembriwriter.yolasite.com/

David Schembri and The Writing Show. Published Fall 2014.

ISBN 978-0-9860304-3-7

Unearthly Fables

DAVID SCHEMBRI

Edited by Paula Berinstein
Foreword by Marty Young

For my family.
Rhonda, Anthony, and Eve.
Without you this wouldn't mean much.

TABLE OF CONTENTS

Foreword by Marty Young 11
Preface by Robert Hood 13
Gaitrel the Black 15
The Seamstress 17
The Spectre 21
Grandma 24
The Arrow 26
World of Amusements 28
Fine Mortal Cabernet 32
The Reaction 34
Nigel's Evening 37

SIGHTINGS IN THE DARK 41
Over the Eyes.. 42
The Prolonging 43
Eat Up... 44
The Noise Upstairs 45
Man of the Parlor.. 46
Night, Night.. 47
Vixen 48
A Way to Conquer Fear 51
On the Seventh Day...52
Wasteland..53
Psycho Circus 54
The Iron Fist 56
Tiny Fish..57
The Water People 59

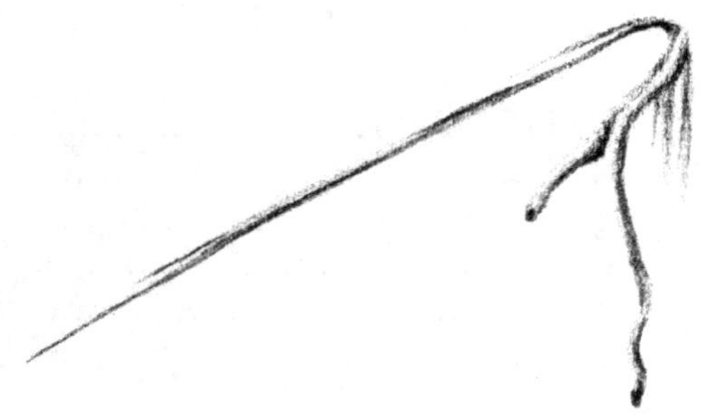

The Tuning of Hex...61
Vow's Passage 75
War of Me 83
Hearts of Winter..86
Despair of the Hunted...89
On the Shards of Broken Glass 92
Touched 98
Soulless 102
Beasts of the Danube Delta....................................105
Parhelion: Rage of the Starborn 108
An Interview with David Schembri by Paula Berinstein... 135

FOREWORD
by Marty Young

When you read Dave Schembri's fiction and study his artwork, you're likely to think he was the deranged, psychotic, axe-wielding bastard child of Freddy Krueger and Elizabeth Báthory, with an intense dislike for humanity—but he's not. He's one of the nicest guys I know, with a truly wacky sense of humour. I can still picture him at the pub during Worldcon in 2010, trying to tell a story but laughing so much that he was crying and barely able to speak. I'm not sure what the story was, but I think it was at his own expense (he's like that). He also plays the guitar and sings. I kind of always thought he'd be a screeching thrash metaller with anger management issues, but nope, I got that wrong too.

Dave lets through some of his wacky humour in *Unearthly Fables* ("Fine Mortal Cabernet" gives you a hint of it, while "Nigel's Evening" is a laugh-out-loud riot, and a break from the grim goodies to either side of it), but for the most part, the tales and art within this collection are dark and terrible. They are pure horror: hapless women giving birth to demons, lurking men with monstrous hearts becoming the victims of things much worse, condemned souls finding a "way" out of hell, and cold-blooded murder directed by horrific creatures.

Sometimes, it's the fine details that get you, like this bit from "World of Amusements:"

The first cuts were a lot of work, but once he had destroyed the garments,
the dismemberment became much more efficient.

There is blood spilt here, oh yes, and lots of it. These are short, sharp tales of revenge—rapid cleaver strokes that maim—but the thing that strikes me most about this motley collection is the morality, even if that moral isn't at first obvious. Dave's fiction tells a story, and it's always one worth reading.

It is quite a skill to construct well-rounded tales in such a few words, and David Schembri is a master. He's got flash fiction nailed. But the true test of a writer's ability is when they extend themselves, and some of the longer pieces here—"The Tuning of Hex" and "Parhelion," for example—prove that he is just as good in those formats as in the shorter ones.

Unearthly Fables contains thirty-four stories, most of them bite-sized nuggets of horror goodness, and nineteen pieces of superb art. It's a collection I can't recommend highly enough. But beware as you venture forth. Don't expect good always to triumph; this is a view of the night-time world—make no mistake about it.

As Dave says, "May the Seamstress have mercy on your souls."

PREFACE
by Robert Hood

David Schembri's *Unearthly Fables* is a darkly evocative Pandora's box of a book.

Made up of compact short-short stories of horror and dark fantasy, a flash fiction collection gathered under the title "Sightings in the Dark," a few longer tales, and a concluding science fiction thriller, *Unearthly Fables* aims to unsettle the reader and leave phantom scratches on the psyche.

The varied collection never seems merely random. Without sharing story continuity or characters, the shorts create a unity of tone and colour, a thematic resonance that is enhanced by the author's evocative illustrations. We feel that we're in a consistent and unsettling world. What the shorts and flash fiction inevitably lack in complex plotting, they make up for in atmosphere and dark imagery, jabs of black humour, half-seen glimpses into strange realities, and moments spent lost in the nastier corners of the human mind. This tonal unity even embraces the concluding more plot-driven SF novella, which has enough grotesque imagery and violent adventure to sit comfortably with and complement the preceding tales of supernatural and visceral horror.

On top of all this, Schembri has asked some of Australia's leading practitioners of the weird tale to write a brief lead-in to the stories—another unusual touch. The book ends with an interview with Schembri conducted by editor Paula Berinstein, exploring the author's thoughts on horror and his own work.

All up, *Unearthly Fables* is a distinctive collection of horror fiction, offering the reader a glimpse into the darker corners of Schembri's imagination.

THE BIRTH

GAITREL THE BLACK

A castle, a fair maiden, a magician . . . but beware of Gaitrel. "Take my hand," he said, then led me to things hidden from the world.

—Amanda J. Spedding, author of the apocalyptic short "The Long Ago," mythology mutation "The Road," and award-winning steampunk story "Shovel-Man Joe"

The young girl's screams echoed within the shadows of the tower. Gaitrel leaned over her and said gently, "Do not despair, child." He tried to calm her with a hand to her forehead, but she continued to cry and fought wearily within the rusted shackles. "There are many wonders in store for you after tonight." He straightened and leaned on his staff. "You are about to become the mother of an immortal child. You will receive a beautiful castle, an order of guards, and perhaps even have a kingdom named after you!" he said.

"Y-you told me I was g-going to die," she spat.

Her saliva sprayed onto his grey beard, and he flinched. Gaitrel bit at his lower lip and slowly recalled her purpose. The events of these past centuries had wreaked havoc on his memory. He could not remember having told her such lies before. He sighed with dismay and peered down at the pale, baggy robes that signified his fall. He was the last of his kind. Alone. Troubled. Practically powerless, and losing his memory was the last thing he wanted. It was all he had. But now . . .

The girl's screams suddenly intensified and he gazed up.

Another was born.

The young demon had burst out of her gut, staining her white night dress with blood and innards. She lay motionless on the stone bed as the demon chewed and bit at her flesh.

Gaitrel stepped towards the newborn. It snarled at him and screamed an insult, complaining that the meat was bitter. He bowed his head, gathered the demon up in his arms, and wrapped its bloody body in his robes. It struggled for a few moments but soon settled and began to slumber noisily in his embrace. Gaitrel sighed again and proceeded with the ritual.

He would raise the demon and live with it. Feed it the flesh of livestock. Cope with the stench of its filth as it lay in steaming heaps around the halls of his tower. Then, a time would come when it would be old enough to depart. To be released into a nearby village. It would assume the form of a local townsman—and wait.

He laid the slumbering beast into a cradle made from iron and lined with straw, and gazed at its flapping lips. His mind continued to show signs of its former strength, supplying images of the tasks that lay ahead. Once the power of his staff had regenerated, he would obtain another young virgin using a seductive scent—a pink haze that would entice her up to his tower.

Gaitrel dragged his feet into the gloom of his chamber and slumped into his throne of ironstone. His staff fell from his grip and rolled noisily onto the floor, the impact echoing in the tall ceilings. He wearily rubbed his sweaty brow and mumbled, "Come, come. Speak to me before I forget where I am."

He sat in the silence for endless moments before shadows swirled around the spines of his books. Soon the voices eddied around his ears.

All ten of his departed order visited him that night, an order he'd led through the Dark Ages before their fall to the Lord's army. Their voices encouraged and worshiped him, despite the faded condition of his robes. The birth of the newborn signaled yet another troop for their impending army of fire. Once the circle of demons was complete, his order would rise again.

Gaitrel looked down at his robes and grinned as the colors grew a shade darker. The time to reshape the way of the world would come, and he would regain his title.

He would no longer be known as the fumbling fool.

He would again be Gaitrel.

Gaitrel the Black.

THE SEAMSTRESS

A lonely woman cannot be too careful. But neither can some predators. Heed a warning inscribed by needles in blood.

—Kyla Lee Ward, author of *The Land of Bad Dreams*

There was a place beneath a haze dark and terrible. Trees stretched into the sky and creeks weaved their way around the hills of a great range. In that wilderness, settlements spread and grew into a lively township—a township where blood flowed through lovely veins.

Living veins.

A hermit, the townsfolk labeled her. A witch? the children wondered fearfully. Perhaps, but for me, the woman was something else: the perfect quarry. She was middle-aged with a full head of wild brown hair. Deterring the locals with glaring looks from her dark, sunken eyes, she walked the damp streets alone in clothing that hung heavily from her thin body like crimson drapes. It was fortunate that this woman was disliked. She would not be missed.

I had taken my usual time studying her movements, and before long, I knew her routine. I chose to begin my hunt after her usual afternoon stroll and followed her back to an old cottage, which thankfully was hidden and secluded. Once she was inside, I emerged from the shield of the overgrown hedge that fronted her property and walked down a cobblestone path to the door, which bore a tarnished lion's head knocker.

THREADS

I tapped until I heard her footsteps. A few locks and dead bolts were released (a lonely woman cannot be too careful), and then the door stood ajar. She peered at me with her pale face, and rolled her eyes with distaste. Fortunately, I am an old and frail man and appear harmless.

"Can I help you?" she snapped.

"Indeed, my dear," I began in a sad voice. "I was wondering if I could use your telephone?"

"Pardon?"

"I am old and foolish and have forgotten my way around these hills. Just one call so I can have my grandson collect me."

"Lost? The town is but a short walk to the east!"

"My arthritis has me stranded, I am afraid. It will take but a moment."

She stared, then sighed and unlocked the door.

She guided me down the hall of her gloomy residence. Some Celtic classical music lingered in the air. The dark carpets exuded a damp smell. The wallpaper was barely visible, being covered almost completely by large and small picture frames holding individual and group portraits. The faces stared back at me as I glided by, all pale, all frozen. The subjects' clothing seemed to place them in past centuries.

"Relations of yours?" I could not help asking.

No answer.

I was led into a dimly lit kitchen where a phone was mounted on the wall beside a potbellied stove. "I will dial the number for you," she grunted.

"It doesn't matter now " I said. It was time for the incursion. Time for the body to be mine.

I approached swiftly, placed my right hand on her pale forehead, and released my soul's hold on my old host. I felt myself slide down from its head, through its arm, and into the very tips of its fingers, ready to enter into a new kingdom of flesh, blood, and life.

What I should have seen was the usual vortex spiraling around me as I dove into my new dominion. I should have tasted the sweet essence of her soul as I absorbed her life force.

No.

Time stood still. Then she spoke.

"Fool. This body is taken. How dare you try and invade my veins. This is *my* bed, *my* blood, you imbecile! Like all of the others, you ride from body to body like a parasite. Do you think the only reason for your existence is to live and keep living? We are the spinners of the flesh, of the souls! We should be the controllers, for the world to see and bow to! I am tired of only being known to those who have been locked up in padded rooms. It is time for us to rise and rule!"

She snatched me into her head. I saw through her eyes the falling of my old body. I was trapped!

Later, she returned me to my old host's body but gave me no privileges. "I am going to make an example out of you," she growled, and banished me onto an old bed in a small dark bedroom, its walls also covered by picture frames. Thousands of faces were looking upon me, all frozen, all stuck in time.

"They are all like you," she began. "They fought at first, but now they exist in the stillness until they are educated. When I feel the time is right, they will become my army. Through you, they shall learn."

From time to time she would enter the room and allow me to move. When I was able to, I revolted—thrashing, cursing—but with a blink of her eyes, I would be paralyzed again, disgraced, humiliated, with thousands of eyes watching, learning the might of their master. For months I lay there, a haven for maggots and flies.

She told me she is the keeper of the Needle of Flesh, the wielder of the Vein Thread. And one by one, she did build her army. Bone built upon bone, joint unto joint, weaved together with blood-filled veins, they stood and were wrapped with a spool of flesh. Her soldiers are not easy on the eyes. They are hideous monstrosities, reborn for a single purpose: to help her gain control of the living world. Their skin is leathery, but over time, it settles and sinks to give them a more acceptable form—one that can walk deceivingly amongst the living.

This is her army, all anointed to new life, all pledged to their mother, my executor.

May the Seamstress have mercy on your souls.

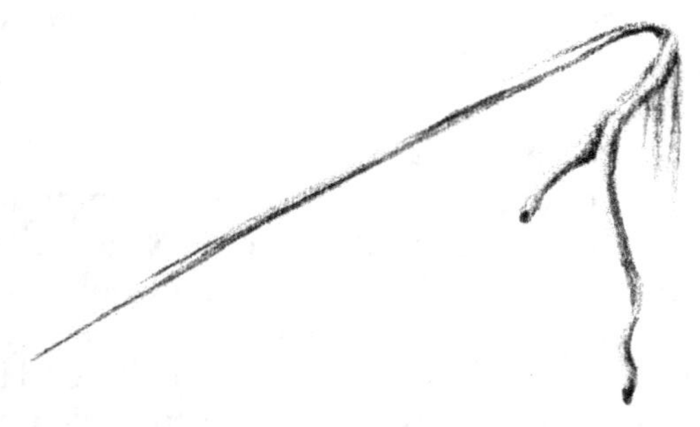

 THE SPECTRE

Everyone agrees it's good to have a purpose in life. But a purpose in death? Some may think twice about that . . .

—Robert Hood, *author of Fragments of a Broken Land: Valarl Undead*

After my death I was confused, dazed and lost, but soon a hunger for revenge lifted my spirit, and gave me a new purpose.
Sit back, and let me enlighten you . . .

The woods were the first thing my dead eyes saw. There was something about the place—something that confused me, as if I'd been there before. I remembered the cold, the same stillness in my chest, and the mist that covered the undergrowth; the mysterious pathways that snaked through the dense scrub, the foreign surrounds—the tall swaying trees that stretched into the clouds, the twilight that beamed down through the canopy. It was all so familiar, but I couldn't make sense of it. Why had my legs, as if having a will of their own and ignoring orders from my mind, brought me here?

At my bare feet lay the bank of a creek, a little stream of rushing, murky water. Wilted shrubs, starved of the sun's goodness, bowed their leaves, and river grasses swayed and danced beneath the surface. My eyes, dry and wide, followed the creek's path, which disappeared into a large drainpipe—so large, in fact, that I could have walked through it. Above the drain was a mud-clad road, the lonely pathway my legs had traveled to bring me to this place that seemed so secret and so still and so foreboding.

Why have you brought me here? I said to my pale, bare legs. No answer. Just the aging branches of the trees creaking eerily in the winds.

A sound broke the silence. Was it a scream? I snapped my gaze up to a muddy road and saw figures. The twilight was deepening, and the bodies that shifted and moved above me were dark and featureless. I took a few steps toward them and felt icy snakes up my back. They were fighting!

A girl who looked not a year over eighteen struggled within the grip of a large man. She was facing away from him, clawing at his thick and hairy arm, which was threatening to crush her throat. Her feet were nearing the edge, and I guessed that it would be no challenge for him to throw her small body into the rushing water below. The rocks would surely injure her skin, her bone—maybe even kill her.

He was a filthy display of a man—overweight, with sweat visible on his large arms, torn jeans, a tattered cap, and a stretched, dark shirt. I saw him reach for something in his belt: a large knife. Even in the darkening light, the blade glinted. This had gone too far. I wanted to do something, *anything*, and ran up to intervene. I screamed at them, but only the birds seemed to hear.

Then the figures noticed me.

Both of them. Victim and eradicator, each confused. They stared in my direction, but their gazes passed me and pierced the woodlands behind where I stood. The man tilted his head, and I could see that he was uneasy. He was still holding the girl, whose long hair was stuck to her round face.

Let the girl go, I said, and immediately he flinched.

Release her, now.

He stepped back, holding his knife out defensively, and I thought I could see his eyes dart, thought I could hear him whimper.

The girl struggled again and managed to free herself. She wasted no time running from him, but he cared little for her escape. He just stood there looking about, as if trying to see whatever it was that he had heard—what he feared—his knife following his search.

I remained still. The girl had disappeared down the muddy road toward safety. He couldn't have caught her now, not with the extra weight he was carrying.

Alone at last.

He flinched again, as if he'd been jabbed through the belly with an invisible poker, and fell into the water, landing hard on the rocks. I peered down and saw him muttering in agony and terror. Blood was spurting from his split nose and spreading across his broken face, and he was trying to stanch the flow with a large, trembling hand. One of his legs was bent unnaturally.

Did that hurt?

As though protecting himself from needles piercing his eyes, he covered his face with his hands and screamed. I stepped to the river bank, and he wailed into the creeping darkness.

You are trapped here with me.

He screamed and swayed, then pulled his hands away and gazed up to where I stood, his eyes full of disbelief and dread, as if staring into the face of something that should not be.

Oh, but I *am* real. I *am* something that cannot be seen but can be heard, and now, seeing you here like this, I know my purpose.

Revenge lifts my spirit.

So I kept telling my murderer until he was dead.

GRANDMA

Heredity can be a bitch, and blood is always thicker than water. Especially when it's all over the kitchen floor. Come and spend a lovely evening at Grandma's house.

—Martin Livings. Martin Livings' first short story collection, Living with the Dead, is now available from Dark Prints Press (http://www.martinlivings.com)

Grandma can be so cranky. I can't see why Mum believes we are so much alike. I do have Grandma's eyes and even her witty smile at times. I like hats like she does. She has many up in her attic, but she never lets me touch them. She never lets me touch anything in her house, come to think of it.

Mum says I will grow to look like her one day. "You have the same jaw line," Mum says.

I shrug. I'd hate to look like Grandma when I'm old. She's all skinny, and her back hunches over in a wicked arch, and her breath smells like ash. Mum says I even have Grandma's walk when I'm tired, and I hate to think of that too.

Grandma puts little white sticks in her mouth and breathes their smoke, and I don't know why. They always make her cough. I can't see myself doing that! Whenever I ask her why she puffs away at them, I hear her croaky voice shout, "I'll do what I want!"

Grandma likes pets, though. I like pets—at least nice ones. Grandma doesn't have nice pets. She has a budgie up in a little yellow cage. His name is Burt. He nips at my fingers with his beak whenever Grandma orders me to fill his water dish. He's a little green noisy thing, and I think he's sick. Some of his feathers are missing here and there, and

I can see grayish skin on the bare patches. Then there's Grandma's cat. Max is his name. He's just as old as Grandma, I think. He snorts when he walks, and bubbles of snot balloon from his nose whenever he sleeps. He always hisses at me, and whenever he does, Grandma always yells, "Leave him alone, child!"

"I didn't do anything to him!" I cry.

"Don't talk back!" she barks again.

So, why are we so alike? I don't think I even like Grandma, but Mum always says sternly, "No, you *love* Grandma."

One night I realized we do have something more in common. I was staying there when Mum needed to go and work late at the hospital. I was hungry up in the room Grandma keeps me in. It smells of old books and Max's wee. I never liked what Grandma gives me for dinner. Yucky fish pie. It stinks and almost makes me cry whenever I smell it being cooked. I smell it even before getting through the front door when Mum drops me off.

So, I was hungry. I knew where Grandma kept her cookies. They were high up in a cupboard in the kitchen, but I knew I could reach them if I used a chair. I crept downstairs and was as quiet as I could be.

Squeak, squeak, the steps went as I tiptoed down. The lights were on in Grandma's room, so I knew she'd gone to bed to puff on her white sticks for a bit. Sometimes she would doze off to the big black and white TV in her lounge room, but luckily for me, it was puff night.

Just when I thought all was going well, Grandma caught me in her kitchen. What was she doing downstairs? Anyway, that didn't matter. She turned the light on and glared at me as I was digging my hand into her cookie jar. I was so scared, I nearly wet my pajamas.

She roared and I screamed. She plucked me down from the chair by twisting my ear. Then she hit me. She does that sometimes. It always hurts. The back of her boney hand struck my face. Once, twice, then a third time.

"Off to bed, you little thief!" she yelled.

I cried. My cheek was throbbing. When she turned away, I gave in to a sudden feeling. I don't know what came over me. Maybe it was because I was getting older. I wanted to hurt her back. I shoved my foot into her hip, sending her plummeting to the hard tile floor.

I kicked her . . . once, twice, and then a third time.

There it was. Not only do I have her eyes, her smile, and liking for pets.

I have Grandma's anger too.

 THE ARROW

Jason thought he had his love life sorted. Then he made a deal with a matchmaker.

—Kaaron Warren, author of seven books including *Slights* and *Through Splintered Walls*

His face was something to remember, pale and layered with sweat as he saw me staring at them through his bedroom window. Luckily, her head was facing the other way so she didn't see him desperately gesturing for me to depart. But, of course, I wasn't going anywhere.

I signaled for him to meet me at his front door, and when he realized that I was serious, he nodded in submission. I made my way around the side of his house, trampling his rose garden (accidentally . . . I promise), and stepped up onto his porch. I listened to his footsteps as they hastily approached, and before I knew it, he had swung the door open.

"Good evening, pig," I greeted him.

"What are you doing here?" he spat in a harsh whisper. He had covered his nakedness with a twisted and sweaty sheet. "How dare you spy on me? Get off my porch!"

"I will, Justin. But, I'm not exactly finished with you . . . yet."

"What? Listen, matchmaker! I paid you to get me a date with her, not to give me counseling! Go away!"

"Oh, yes. Your 'date.' How long will it last, pig? If I know your style, you'll boot her out before breakfast."

"Stop calling me that! So I'm a womanizer! It's none of your business!"

Quite the contrary," I huffed.

In no more than a blink of an eye, I gave the swine a glimpse. I spread my white wings and allowed my skin to glow. His eyes widened in wonder.

"Wha-what?" he gasped as tears streamed down his cheeks. "Cu-Cupid? You are Cupid?" he muttered.

"Congratulations! Your eyes work! Now, how about your heart?"

"What do you mean?"

"Come on, Justin. You're a sleaze bag. Those days are over. It's time for love now."

"Love? I don't want love! I just—"

"Sorry, dear boy. It's too late. I'm in charge of your destiny now."

"B-b-but love hurts!" he wept.

"Fear not. Love is also tender, warm, and devoted. You'll see."

With that, I pulled out one of my gold-headed arrows, readied my bow, and shot him straight through the heart.

I stepped over him as he lay twitching on his back. My arrow had absorbed into his chest and was beginning to do its magic. He looked at me with terror in his eyes. "What if she doesn't return my l-love?" he cried.

I knelt down to him and said gently, "That's the chance you take."

WORLD OF AMUSEMENTS

Treat others as you wish to be treated. It's an old saying, but one Anna and Julie should have heeded. Doesn't matter whether you're the most beautiful in school, or the most popular. If you treat people like dirt, eventually it'll come back to burn you.

—Brett McBean, author of *The Mother, The Awakening,* and *Tales of Sin and Madness*

Gerald orchestrated everything so it would take place late, after the carnival's business hours. Sitting within the confines of the attraction, biting his nails, he made sure everything was well insulated, to muffle any noise. His family had retired for the evening in a nearby settlement, ten minutes away on foot. They wouldn't hear a thing.

"It will happen," he thought in the darkness, and it did. As he'd planned, they slid down, the two of them. The intense, spiraling descent within the tube slide ended with a deep drop, and Gerald had removed the safety net for the occasion.

He gasped with anticipation, and within a heartbeat, it was over. The girls hit the solid ground like two rolling lumps. Gerald approached through the settling dust and stared down at Anna and Julie. Their heads sat unnaturally upon their shoulders, and their lifeless eyes stared into the nothingness around them. Gerald grinned before grabbing their legs.

He gazed down at their beauty. Anna and Julie's hair looked well styled, and if there was a current fashion, they seemed to be wearing it. He did not know of such things, as his life consisted of selling tickets at the carnival and reluctantly attending Greenwood High School, where he was tormented on a daily basis.

He had enjoyed constructing his plan. It hadn't taken much. He had tricked them with an invitation that looked to have come from their boyfriends. It read:

Meet us at the Greenwood Carnival! Go to the attraction with the balloons outside! When you get to the bottom, we'll be waiting!
Lots of love, Todd & Casey

Gerald was used to seeing the girls in their cheerleading outfits or their regular school uniforms, and their "fuck me" clothes disgusted him. "So this is how you look when you meet up with boys," he muttered as he dragged them out of the tube slide's enclosure.

Because he was larger than most sixteen-year-olds, it wasn't a difficult heave. Gerald wanted to be the muscle man of the carnival one day, like his Uncle Gordon. "I will get there," he thought as he towed the two limp girls towards the carnival's main attraction.

"Ellister," he breathed as he approached the carnival's steam engine, the reason they remained open for business. She was the only existing shunting locomotive in the United States, purchased by his great grandfather (the carnival's founder), or so the story went. Gerald had always been fascinated with Ellister and the four cars she towed. She had been circling the carnival and pleasing their patrons for more than eighty years. He had been assisting Ellister's driver, cousin Max, ever since he was seven. Gerald was never allowed to drive Ellister, no matter how often he'd protest to his cousin. Max would preach, with his sweaty cigarette squeezed between his teeth, "Driving a flying arrow is a dangerous business, lad. If you don't keep Ellister's boiler happy, you're in for one mean explosion!"

The one thing Gerald had been allowed to learn, however, was how to fuel Ellister's fire box.

Gerald guessed the fire had grown to the right temperature and dropped the girls before Ellister's cabin. He narrowed his eyes to fend off the orange heat from within. Staring down at the two beauties for the last time, he pulled them up one by one, dumping them on the cabin floor, then picked up the machete he had borrowed from the carnival's small museum, took a breath, and began to swing.

The first cuts were a lot of work, but once he had destroyed the garments, the dismemberment became much more efficient. When finished, he quickly opened the fire box door. The hot, acrid smoke ate at his cheeks as he fed the fire and listened to the red coals feasting and crackling. He stared down at the remaining piece: Anna's head.

He picked it up gently and rested it in the fire. "You were the worst," he muttered as he stared into her dead gaze. He balled his hands into fists. He remembered her southern voice yelling, "Stay away from me, you fat, retarded freak!"

Everyone in the cafeteria had looked his way. Julie had laughed, sealing her own fate. That incident still hurt him, like all the others.

"No more," Gerald exclaimed as tears formed in his eyes.

Satisfied with the incineration, Gerald made his way back through the night. He entered the enclosure of the carnival's tube slide; the balloons still hung from its entrance. He checked his wristwatch, calmed his breathing, and waited.

He had issued more than one invitation.

Todd and Casey were due to arrive soon.

GERALD AND THE CHEERLEADERS

FINE MORTAL CABERNET

When vampires host a party, mere mortals get drunk! This eloquent wine label describes a drop of red that's to die for.

—Cameron Trost, author of Hoffman's Creeper and Other Disturbing Tales

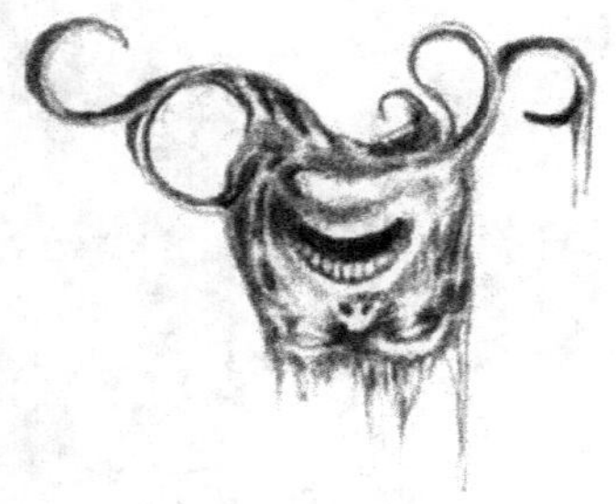

Fine Mortal Cabernet
(1866)

This is a glorious, thick ruby-red drop which shows an intense syrupy nose, with layers of leather and a hint of iron and earthiness. It is mouth-filling and succulent, with flavours of lead and balanced beautifully with its natural acids. Its texture is firm yet silky on the palate.

Vintage human.

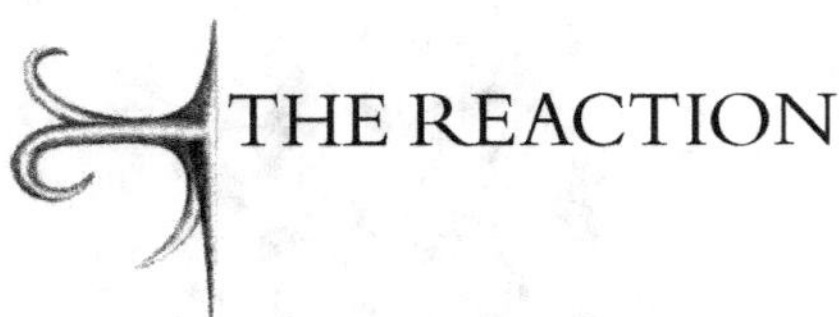

THE REACTION

David's excursion into the question of nature vs. nurture is one that Sharon and Aaron wish he'd never taken.

—Juliet Bathory, editor of Andromeda Spaceways Inflight Magazine, *Issue 48,* co-editor of *Andromeda Spaceways Inflight Magazine Best of Horror Volume 2,* and layout designer for *Midnight Echo Magazine*

Aaron snatched his towel from the rack. A morning chill goosed his flesh as he wrapped himself in the soft fabric. He patted his chest dry, trying to capture the dying warmth of the steam.

As he stepped out onto the bathmat, his wife, Sharon, awaited him, her arms crossed. She stared at him with half-awake eyes. "You know," she said, "you're not going anywhere until I've looked at that arm."

"I'll be fine," Aaron muttered, and dried his legs. His arm was still aching.

"I'll be the judge of that," Sharon said. She gestured for him to stand. "Come on, give me a look."

"It hardly hurts anymore," Aaron said as he stood. Reluctantly, he held out his arm for inspection. "See, the blisters have gone, and the lump is down. I've been stung before, you know."

"It's still red! Does your arm feel tight? Can you move it properly?"

"Yeah, yeah. It'll be fine," he said, unwilling to jeopardize his weekly golf trip.

"Did you see what stung you? It must have been big enough to notice. I can *still* see the hole where the stinger went in."

"Nah, I didn't get a good look at it. I brushed it off my arm when I felt it. It probably flew away to die somewhere. Maybe a wasp? Something

THE REACTION

like that. There was word of some hives down by the refinery's garden. That would explain where it came from."

Sharon stepped back and her eyes narrowed. She had never liked the company he worked for. "You should make a claim on Work Cover. That bloody place has a responsibility!"

"Yeah, I know," Aaron sighed. "I would, but it was a stressful morning, and I *really* needed a smoke. I didn't actually take an allocated break—"

"Oh, bloody hell, Aaron!"

"I know. Stuff happens. I'll be all right," he reassured her, rubbing his arm.

"Aaron, you play golf every week. I'm sure your buddies can live without you for today. You should rest your arm."

"No. Being lazy isn't going to help. The fresh air will do me good." Aaron relaxed his expression and placed a gentle hand on Sharon's face.

She flinched immediately and screeched, as if hit by a sudden surge of pain.

"Shaz!" Aaron bellowed.

Sharon clasped her hands to her face. She stumbled and fell to her knees.

Aaron froze where he stood. He tried shrieking, but he'd become deaf and mute. He watched Sharon sink to the floor, her eyes glazing over, her consciousness fading, till she was still.

Moments later, Aaron was able to lift a shaking hand before his face. His terrified eyes saw the stingers as they retracted beneath his fingernails.

Tears formed in his eyes.

Sharon's head swelled rapidly, doubling in size while Aaron's soul withered away to nothing, and the emerging monstrosity grinned, longing for more.

NIGEL'S EVENING

Nigel's life is full of disappointment, triumph, and envy. Within the gloomy alley, will downtrodden Nigel take his opportunity to shine? David offers the reader a glance into one decisive moment of Nigel's life.

—Rhonda Schembri, critic of life, participant in nature, and observer of humanity

The chills he felt beneath his flesh were more from excitement than fear.

Nigel concealed himself behind the dumpster. Shrouded within the late gloom of the dingy alley, he held out the handy cam and directed its lens. It was the office's loan model and the viewscreen didn't work, but it would do the job.

He glided his thumb over the zoom toggle.

Finally, it was going to be his night. For years he'd been stuck behind his desk inducting young bloods into the *Weekly Herald*, watching them rise above him, settling into offices he so longingly wanted to occupy. Year after year he was overlooked for promotion. A klutz, they called him, but he was determined to prove them wrong.

This night, it was his time to shine.

As he hid behind the rancid-smelling dumpster, the goods were finally at his fingertips. A local senator and a known crime figure were meeting and shaking hands. He would have the evidence on digital video. He knew he was not within range to capture voices, but the images would be enough to confirm his story.

Thinking excitedly about his future, he kept the camera as still

NIGEL

as he could. No more disappointed glances from his wife. No more disinterested expressions from his offspring. No more endless days slouched behind a desk.

"I'm gonna be famous!" he snickered.

The minutes rolled by. Nigel peered around the corner of the dumpster and watched the secret meeting conclude. He waited, the steam of his ambition clouding his face. He heard cars disappear into the night. He ran from the gloom of the alley and rested his back on the street corner and gasped with excitement. He set the handy cam to rewind. It vibrated in his shaking hands, and he clenched his teeth in anticipation.

Click! He pressed "Play."

Nigel watched the footage for a few seconds before hurling the handy cam onto the pavement.

He had recorded four minutes of the lens cap.

THE ANSWER

 SIGHTINGS IN THE DARK

A Flash Fiction Collection

What's that up ahead? It's dark—too dark to see clearly—but you can see flashes of something disturbing: a proactive mortician, a cop facing his worst nightmare, a grisly circus act. As your eyes adjust to the gloom, the details become clearer and the subtle becomes more obvious: the misanthropy, the aggression, and even the wry humour. These are the Sightings in the Dark, and when you truly see that which lies in the darkness, you may want to tear your eyeballs out.

—Shane Jiraiya Cummings, author of *Shards,* the *Apocrypha Sequence,* and *The Abandonment of Grace and Everything After*

OVER THE EYES

"You're not the only one. I want the leader."

The girl stared blankly at him, mascara smudged beneath her eyes. He took another drag from his cigarette.

"You won't go to juvenile detention. You'll be charged as an adult. We don't deal with hate crimes lightly. Don't take this on yourself. Give up the leader."

Silence. She gestured with her middle finger.

He laughed. "The inmates are gonna eat you alive." He extinguished his fag and slid a pad and pencil over to her side of the table. "The leader. You may get out of this with time to start over."

She stared at the paper. An hour later, she scribbled.

The detective snatched it. He gasped.

He was staring at his daughter's mobile number.

THE PROLONGING

"You can walk!"

Her grandfather halted, his face pale with terror. She stormed out, and he stood frozen.

He ran to find her, only to be thrown to the floorboards.

She broke both of his legs with a sledge hammer. "I worked double shifts to pay for that wheelchair, and I'm going to get my money's worth!"

EAT UP

"Now then, you haven't got any squealing little birds by your side, so no regurgitation this time. Mummy wants you to eat up your dinner, okay?"

Her son nodded eagerly, his fork and knife held tightly in each hand. The mother smiled proudly and dropped the screaming morsel into his bowl.

He gobbled it up quickly, like the good little giant he was.

THE NOISE UPSTAIRS

Andy hid beneath the stairs. The familiar creaks sent shivers up her spine. She knew it was useless; he always found her.

As each stair squeaked beneath the weight of his energy, Andy hugged her legs in the darkness.

Her late father always radiated blue in the moonlight, which beamed through the front window. It would have been beautiful under other circumstances.

She gasped as he approached.

The white orbs of his eyes stared. He motioned a transparent hand over the scars on her arm, goosing her flesh.

"Wasn't torturing me in your living years enough?" she said.

"Not a chance. Obession never dies."

MAN OF THE PARLOR

Marcel tipped the young boy and watched him scurry off into the night. Stepping inside, he huffed at the overdue bills pinned to his door. His wife entered, bringing him a steaming cup of tea.

"Has there been word?"

"Yep. The Corelly brothers know of their sister's murder."

"Have they blamed the Zamitt family?"

He nodded, winked, and accepted the cup. "There's going to be a war on the streets by sunrise."

Marcel opened the doors of his funeral parlor and gazed at the empty pews.

"You'd best get your account book ready. We are going to get very busy."

NIGHT, NIGHT

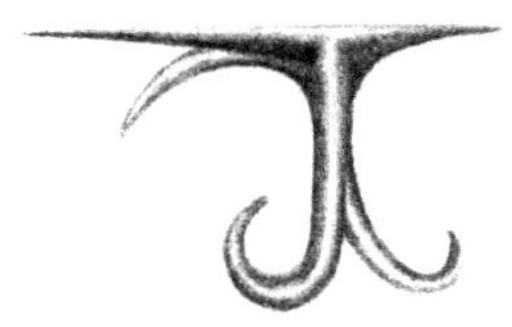

"I will not wait until a burn on your arm teaches you not to touch the hot water tap!" the father grumbled as he tucked the blankets beneath the mattress. He kissed his son gently upon the forehead before turning off the lamp.

"Night, night," the father whispered. He retrieved his simmering cigarette from off the nightstand. Drawing a deep breath of smoke into his lungs, he left with a cloud in tow.

Alex trembled in the darkness, enduring the throbbing pain that pulsed through his broken wrist.

He hated it when Daddy got mad.

VIXEN

The step out from behind the curtains was an emotional one. The aisle stretched before her, the pathway to her battle ground, where the thundering crowd still gave her gooseflesh. Underneath the screams of the disappointed fans, she could sense a faint vibration from those still loyal. Her face was frozen, and her shiny, tight-fitting pink costume glistened in the lightning of camera fire. She had slicked back her long, dark brown hair into a ponytail adorned with silver glitter. She was Vixen, the former female WCW champion, and she was as shiny and new as the day she'd burst onto the scene. Oh yes, she was a roaring fire in her heyday, but now she was paid even more to submit to her opponents.

She entered the ring and faced her competition, the rising star. Storm was the new fashion. She reminded Vixen of herself in her younger years, fresh and vigorous. Her dark tights, glistening boots, insolent smile, and wild hair appealed to the growing fan base. Although Vixen was only a few years her senior, her style was now past and she felt old. Very old.

The piercing bell rang, and the rehearsed pirouette of aerial combat and body buckling began.

CONFRONTATION

They were alone in the darkness of the private parking lot beneath the stadium. Vixen approached. Her boot heels echoed upon the concrete. Pillar after pillar she drew nearer to Storm's back. Her hands formed into fists, forcing her knuckles white.

"You humiliated me!" Vixen screamed, her voice breaking with fury.

"Get over it!" Storm spat, unlocking her black Hummer.

Vixen stepped closer attempting to calm her rage with a deep breath.

Talk . . . I'm just here to talk.

"That slap wasn't in the script, rookie! You were supposed to pin me down, and that's all!" Vixen growled.

"The crowd loved it! You were out cold anyway. I didn't think you'd even notice!" Storm smirked, boastfully flicking her yellow hair.

Vixen's eye twitched. *Out? Your reverse power slam didn't hit me that hard!*

"You only slapped me because you knew I couldn't do anything about it, you bitch."

"So I improvised. So what?" Storm shrugged. She faced Vixen and chewed her gum loudly. Stepping forward, she spat the gum into Vixen's face. It bounced off her sweaty forehead. She watched it fall from her face and bounce upon the concrete as if it happened in slow motion.

Vixen had forgotten her vow simply to talk. She lifted a skillful foot up and kicked Storm's chin, sending her back into her vehicle. Storm collapsed to the ground. Vixen stepped over her and nudged Storm's leg with her foot.

Out cold.

"Improvise? Two can play at that game, sweetheart."

A WAY TO CONQUER FEAR

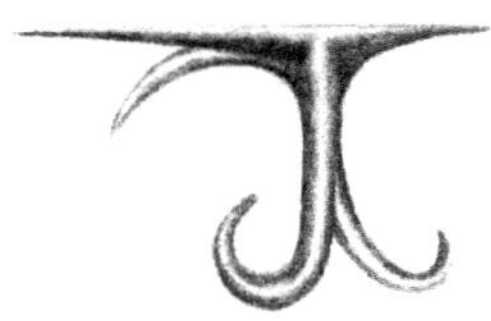

I clutched at the bars. Gravity was winning, sucking me closer as if some enormous giant were breathing me in. I cried out, but no one heard. No one but the unseen things beneath me. *Horrible things.* My mind painted images of skeletal hands grabbing at my feet. I cried out! Again and again.

My hands failed me. I fell into the dark. My feet hit, and all was suddenly bright. My eyes opened. Was it a nightmare?

My father hugged me proudly. I did it! I had jumped from the monkey bars.

All by myself.

ON THE SEVENTH DAY

"The evolution is complete. You are finished!"

Adam rose and gazed at his perfect fingers. Eve stroked the silky strands of her golden hair as she lay in the lush, green grass of Eden.

"How did you create us?" asked Adam in wonder.

"With all the love in my heart . . . and a little help from the ape," said God.

"Ape?" they gasped in unison.

God knelt down to them. "Hush now, children," he whispered. "Let us keep that part to ourselves."

They grinned with their fingers crossed behind their backs.

WASTELAND

It's cold in space. Very cold. They'll never tell you that, of course. They'll trick you with promises of adventure and exploration, but what you'll end up with is *this*: abandonment. Priority will be given to the rock samples when the space modules' weight limit is exceeded.

We'll pick you up on our next voyage, they'll say. So (like me) you'll be left alone. Here. On this forsaken planet. A world that has mysteriously orbited ours for centuries. *There was life here once! Oceans and landmass!* they'll promise. But hardly.

I'd bet my left two tentacles on it!

PSYCHO CIRCUS

Snap.
The safety net was cut.
Tremble.
"What are you doing? Are y-y-you mad?"
"I would concentrate if I were you! This is not a rehearsal anymore."
Jitter.
"Leave me be!"
"The higher you go, the farther you'll fall, ya know?"
Shake.
"Shut up!"
"The harder you'll hit, too . . . "
Shudder. Wobble. Rock. Sway.
He smirked as he watched the man plummet.

After the dust settled, the ringmaster stood over him. The broken tightrope walker was frozen, his balancing pole snapped in fragments around him. His mouth was wide with shock. He was still breathing. . . scarcely.

"You stubborn old man. Like I said, I have younger performers ready to take your place. You should have taken the money when you had the chance," he sighed.

Spit. Shake. Quiver.

"Who knows?" he began as he straightened his coat. "Perhaps you'll be dead before I give you to the lions."

RINGMASTER

THE IRON FIST

Bred in the Bronx, fighting ever since puberty, they called me the Iron Fist even after my comeback. I was spectacular, you know, though it cost me. My crooked nose. The gaps in my smile. The dizziness because of these ghosts on my brain. That young punk did all of it. During sleepless nights, I hungered to fight him again.

I was too old, my coach would bark.

But finally, the night came. I had the punk bleeding at my feet in the second round, and the crowd chanted my name.

They called me the Iron Fist, and I still have the bronze in my gloves to prove it.

TINY FISH

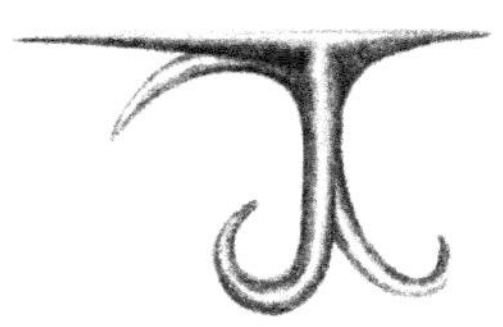

A pair of haunted eyes peers out through the deep gloom. Beneath the waves, schools of fish dart this way and that, and a large ravenous creature emerges from its murky home, pinning its sights on potential prey. His enormous shadow looms over a swiftly swimming morsel, who stares up at him curiously.

"Hello!" the hunter booms. "Are you my lunch?"

"No, I'm not your lunch!" the scrawny voice blurts back.

"Are you sure you're not my lunch? You *do* look tasty!" the hunter booms again, before surging forward and producing an enormous grin of jagged, rotting teeth.

"I'm from the environmental agency!" the tiny fish begins. "There have been complaints around the sea floor about the hazardous products around your home."

The large hunter is shocked, almost offended; he loves his deep-water burrow. "There's nothing wrong with my home," he whimpers.

The teeny fish peers over the hunter's dark scales, and out towards the murky lair. An array of floating bones and fish fragments litters the surrounding reef. His itsy-bitsy eyes peer up at the embarrassed smile of the hunter, who looks upon him as he would any stupid creature. "You give me no choice," his eensy voice barks. "I will have to summon you for a number of violations!"

The bite-sized fish then reveals a miniature clipboard and begins to jot down his notes, reprimanding as he does so. "Summons for pollution! Summons for reckless disposal of waste products! Summons! Summons!

SUMMONS! You are ordered to appear before the tribunal of the reef counci—"

Slurp!

The hunter gulps. He casually conceals the little-bitty's clipboard beneath a nearby rock whilst darting his eyes for any onlookers. As usual, there are none. He slowly swims back to his burrow wearing a smug smile.

They taste so much better when he toys with them first.

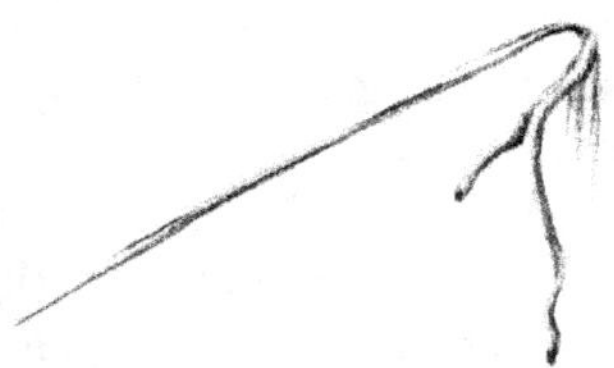

THE WATER PEOPLE

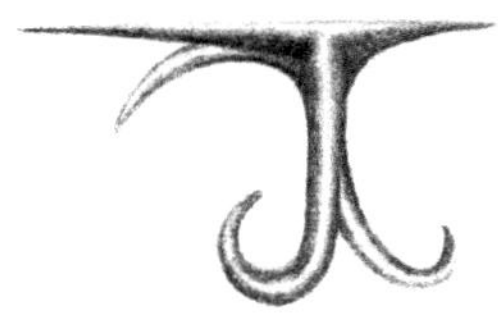

Ivan had already dismissed many passionate people from the factory, and more were to follow. As was his custom, he arrived early, before the others, to get a head start on the day. Sighing, he set his cup beneath the tap of the water filter, filled it until it overflowed, and gulped down the liquid.

Ivan had spent years being "the man on the spot," and this particular takeover was just another devouring. "Heads are gonna roll," he muttered with grim satisfaction.

People thought of him as an assassin, but he didn't care. It was his job, and he was thick-skinned enough to be successful at it. He'd received his fair share of death threats in his time: notes left in his briefcase or slipped beneath the windscreen wipers of his Mercedes Benz, not to mention the nasty emails he would find on his laptop. But none of them had come to anything. "Pathetic!" he would huff. He enjoyed being feared. Not only did he like the power; he fed on it.

Wiping his lips, he grabbed a teaspoon and dumped a heap of coffee into his cup, followed by three servings of sugar. But before reaching for the old kettle, he paused.

In the glare of the office kitchen, something had caught his eye. A small white card rested on top of the water filter. He snatched it and inspected the neatly printed type, which was set beneath a tiny graphic of a water drop. The size of the typography forced him to squint as he read it.

Your water filter system has been serviced this week by The Water People.

You may notice some cloudiness in the water at first. This is oxygen being released from the carbon, and some other ingredients I've added.

If you're feeling some discomfort in your chest right now, try to remember how you sacked me after twenty years of service!

Bile suddenly burning the back of his throat, Ivan gasped and dropped the card. His cup fell from his grasp and shattered at his feet. His heart thudded painfully as he tottered out of the kitchen, the broken porcelain crunching beneath his leather shoes. A cold sweat covered every inch of his body, sticking his expensive threads to his flesh.

He needed to call somebody . . . anybody. He needed help.

Ivan was dead before he got to his desk.

THE TUNING OF HEX

Ever wondered if bad things happen for a reason, and whether senseless death might serve a purpose? David Schembri takes us on a dark, twisted journey between two parallel but intertwined worlds, where misery in one is strength in another, and where even hope is a distorted outcome.

—David Conyers, author of *The Eye of Infinity* and *The Spiraling Worm*

HEX

Through great doorways, they travel,
Invisible, they change destinies.
They are the unseen givers of bad luck.

Across the dark landscape of the parallel world, mountains stretch into the angry sky. Beneath those great giants of rock and stone, there are tunnels and caves—homes of the immortal beings, whose world is a transparent layer coexisting with the mortal presence on Earth. The mortals, living their short, bustling lives with their planes, automobiles, concrete buildings and greenhouse gases, are unaware of the superior others that exist around them.

These beings of the parallel world are called Fate Shifters. They look like Neanderthals and live within the gloom of their caves. There, they can listen to mortals using only the strength of their minds. They call this listening ability "tuning." They rest on beds of stone, and while slumbering, observe mortal activities.

Why do such superior beings listen to inferior creatures? They listen because they must. The foolish mortals are injuring the earth with their pollution, their wars. The Fate Shifters feel the blast of every atom bomb and the devastating quakes it sends through the harrows and forests of their world.

The Fate Shifters have noticed through centuries of observation that whenever a mortal dies in an accident, but not by murder or natural causes, the great mountains of the parallel world grow and strengthen, repairing the damage the mortals are causing. And they've realized that they can use this phenomenon to advantage.

One day an elder of the Fate Shifters came forward and united his people in a quest—a quest to save the earth that the two worlds share, an earth that would take both worlds with it if it were destroyed. He assigned each Fate Shifter a quadrant of the mortal world and ordered them to influence and change the events of certain mortal lives. The philosophy was simple: cause accidents so mortals die and the mountains grow. Execution was difficult, however, and painful. Fate Shifters had to concentrate in short, excruciating bursts in order to create the quick doorways in their sky through which they could enter the world of the mortals. But eventually, when the great giants of rock and stone breached the angry sky, the doorways would become permanent. Then and only then could the Fate Shifters merge the two worlds and affect the mortals.

Educate them. Save them. And if necessary, destroy them.

Friday, October 24th. The Mortal World.

"Well, it has been a pretty good week," Damien Roberts said, taking another large gulp of Victorian Bitters and setting the can back down onto his desk. "We've got all the press approvals signed, all urgent proofs delivered to our customers, and we have all the materials lined up for the guys on the weekend," he continued confidently, giving his tie a quick flick.

"Touch wood," Michael Waley muttered, peering at his manager over his beer can. He took a sip and grimaced as he shifted the warm lager in his mouth, imagining that cat's urine would probably taste sweeter.

"Nah. We have this week in the bag," Damien affirmed, dismissing Michael's doubts with a wave of his hand. "Especially because we just printed that urgent over-label. We have the delivery planned for tonight, and that will keep our client happy. And besides, it's Friday night, for Pete's sake!" he said as he finished his beer.

"Things can still go belly up, you know. There's a lot riding on this delivery. If it fails, we'd best start searching through the job listings," Michael said.

"You're paranoid. You need to be more positive, Mick. Come on, say it with me: *We're gonna be fine.*"

Michael shrugged his shoulders, feeling he would rather be driving to his local pub than be subjected to the waffle that went on after hours during beer-o-clock Fridays. He never used to mind having a cold one with the boys at the end of the week, but things had changed since his promotion. His time was always taken up by the work-obsessed managers, and his old workmates seemed to keep their distance, especially once he had risen in rank. He sighed mournfully as Damien rose from his leather desk chair and reached for his coat.

"Come on, Mick. Let's hear it."

Michael sighed, feeling a familiar dread within his gut. Was it the bad lager, the stress, or cancer? He could never be sure, but whenever he would utter anything sounding the least bit confident, something in his stomach would turn. As if something were stirring in its sleep . . . listening.

"Let's hear it, Mick," Damien said again.

"Fine," Michael said. "We're gonna be fine."

Friday, October 24th. The Parallel World.

"What! Who said that?" yelled Hex, startled by the voices that echoed above him. Tossing his hairy head from side to side in the gloom, he stared wildly up at the cave's ceiling, searching for them. High above him, he could hear the reverb of distant words, blaring out from one of the many tunnels, all of which stretched out into darkness.

Rising from his bed of stones, he dusted the thick fur that covered his legs and torso and leaped towards his cave's ceiling. Soaring through the gloom, he flew into the tunnel from which the voices were coming. The further the darkness swallowed him, the louder the voices became. They spoke of impending fortune, future successes. Every word made him quiver with excitement.

His eyes widened as he caught sight of the exit gaping before him. When he reached the end, the voices became deafening, and he roared. His jaws dried in the rushing wind as a vast red sky welcomed him.

Spreading his arms out like the wings of an eagle, he soared over his world. Red and orange clouds drifted above him as he eyed the black mountains below, and he searched. Once he had caught sight of his master, he channeled his mind, hoping that his master would hear him. "Talon!" Hex's thoughts yelled. "Talon! I need a doorway! I have him!"

As he resettled his large buttocks upon the ledge overlooking the abyss, Talon rolled his eyes at the disturbance in his head. "Not him again," he moaned. He sighed deeply, hoping that the calls of the inexperienced Fate Shifter would disappear, but they continued to wail inside his head. What Talon despised most of all was not Hex himself, but his timing; he always seemed to want something when Talon was just settling down for a rest.

Talon huffed through his thick lips and brushed a few strands of his fur from his grey face, which was webbed with deep wrinkles. He crossed his legs and gazed up at the red sky. Once he caught sight of Hex circling high above the mountain, his eyes narrowed. "What is it?" Talon asked.

"I have him! I need a doorway! Please, master," Hex pleaded.

Talon sighed, knowing where the appeal was leading. Surrendering to Hex's constant pleas, he slammed his eyes shut and focused on the sea in his mind. An ocean of conversations cluttered his search as he tried to locate the cause of the young Fate Shifter's excitement. Diving further into the human din and concentrating his attention, he was able to find Hex's target. Talon's brow furrowed with disappointment, and he shook his head. "You really need to improve your tuning, Hex. Not this pitiful case again. This will have no positive effect on the growth of our world." He rubbed his fleshy brow. "Go home."

"No! Don't send me back to my cave. Not yet. If you want me to learn, then give me the doorway—please. How else am I going to develop my powers if you always send me home?" Hex cried.

"I can't keep letting you indulge in this *Michael* person. You have been asking for more of this ever since you learned the invisibility trick. It's becoming embarrassing. There are younger and brighter Fate Shifters who are tuning more effectively than you and homing in on better subjects. They understand that every twist of fate we achieve that leads to a mortal's accidental death will grow our mountains. They laugh at you. You are falling behind. We want to pierce the sky in *this* century, Hex. Open our world permanently into theirs. That will not happen if you persist with the tiny matters of this *Michael*. The effect will grow only a pebble, not a mountain. I am almost ready to give up on you, so go home."

"No. I will not. I must not. I am tired of the gloom of my cave. Michael is the only one I can hear clearly. That must mean something. Please. It must."

Talon sighed again and thought. If he let Hex go, at least he'd get some peace. "Fine, Hex," he said. "But this is the last time I will release you—unless, of course, your tuning improves. Fail me again and you will be stacking rocks for an eternity," Talon warned as he narrowed his eyes in concentration. "Look to the east. A doorway will open for you."

"Oh, thank you! I will not let you down, I promise!" Hex yelled joyfully, clapping his large hands and spiraling in the sky. "What can I use to change his fate this time?" he asked as he began flying into the eastern clouds.

Talon concentrated reluctantly, grunting through the meaningless babble of Hex's find. He couldn't help feeling sorry for the man Hex kept pursuing. It was because of Hex that the poor mortal had lost several work placements and was about to lose his family. Talon couldn't help thinking the only reason that the mortal world *had* a Michael Waley was so Hex could taunt him with a string of bad luck. Talon sighed and tuned.

"Once you pass through the doorway, you will enter his city. Dive down towards the south, and an address will illuminate beneath you. Something is supposed to happen there which you must prevent. If you wish his fate to change *again,* you must stop the machine."

"Thank you, master," Hex yelled as he saw the bright doorway of light shining from out of a red cloud. "I will return when I can," he called.

"You will return in five minutes!" Talon yelled, and ended his communication, leaving Hex, who was just about to be swallowed by the sky, in a panic.

As his master had predicted, a blue highlight known only to Fate Shifters contoured the buildings below, and Hex descended towards them. The doorway shrank behind him and blended in with the sea of stars. He landed in an industrial park within the shadow of a warehouse. The light was dim; it was that time of night when crickets called from their hiding places. He had been studying the mortal Earth for decades and had always admired the aromas of nature. The sweet smell of small native trees bordering the side of the large block tickled his nostrils. Hex looked about the car park behind him and saw just a few scattered vehicles. He stepped quickly to the corner of the warehouse, concealing his enormous frame behind an aging pine.

Taking a look down the driveway that stretched the length of the building, he could see that it ended at a main road that was busy with nighttime traffic. Hex grinned when he noticed a delivery truck with a blue glow haloing the edges of its tailgate. The truck was parked outside a large dispatch doorway. A forklift was driving in and out, loading large pallets into the rear of the truck. A weary driver stood on the sidelines with his notebook, logging in the load. Hex observed for a few seconds, and then his mind tuned.

We have the delivery planned for tonight, and that will keep our client happy. Hex's brow furrowed as he tuned harder. *There's a lot riding on this delivery. If it fails, we'd best start searching through the job listings.*

Hex sighed with a smile as he realized what he needed to do. Staring at the forklift as it made the last of its loading drives, he filled his large chest with air. His hairy torso swelled, and he arched his back. Holding the breath within his mouth and ballooning his cheeks, he felt his fur stand to attention. A chill covered every inch of his body. Hex tiptoed down the driveway a few steps and gazed at a window to his side.

He could not see his reflection.

Satisfied that he was invisible, he continued his advance on the truck, which was already being closed up by the driver. Once within range, he was startled by the large roller door as it made its noisy descent towards the concrete. The driver had already entered the cabin and had begun to crank the engine. Time was running out.

Hex began to panic. As his first instinct was to injure the driver, he needed to think quickly. His heart pounded.

The engine started.

Struggling to hold his breath, Hex raced to the side of the truck, dropped to his knees, and rolled beneath the engine bay. He was relieved to find that there was enough room between ground and machine for him to maneuver, so he went to work. Imagining that his face had turned purple, Hex released the air from his mouth and removed the cover of his invisibility. He desperately grabbed and pulled at the brake assembly and its cables. When he heard a snap and the sounds of malfunction, he gave a small laugh of triumph.

The driver moved off, luckily too tired to care about the odd sounds of his aging truck, and the instant he was exposed, Hex made for the sky. He soared up high enough not to be noticed by mortal eyes, but not too high, so he could look down at his handiwork. Hovering under the stars, he peered down at the truck as it made its way to the end of the driveway. He clenched his teeth and waited. His eyes dodged back and forth from the truck to the busy nighttime traffic. He let out a shrill of excitement when the truck wouldn't stop.

It rolled out helplessly onto the road.

Hex heard the screeching of wheels, the sounding of horns, and then finally, the collisions. A four-car pileup shattered the peace, but what excited Hex more was that another truck had also crashed. When it made its devastating contact with the cars in front of it, the force caused Hex's truck to roll onto its side. The icing on the cake came when the delivery truck burst into flames.

"There goes *that* delivery," he chuckled.

Doing a quick somersault and throwing his fists around in elation, Hex turned and soared back into the opening doorway of light and vanished.

Upon his bed of rocks, deep within the gloom of his cave, Hex slept happily that night. His dreams were filled with visions of the misfortune he had created. All had gone the way he had hoped. Turning on his bed of rocks, he could hear eruptions from the outside world. Beyond his cave, rocks were moving. Mountains were growing.

Hex smiled proudly.

Saturday, April 14th. The Mortal World.

Taking the last bite from the stale chicken sandwich he had bought from the snack bar, Michael Waley watched as his passengers entered the coach. He sat wearily in a booth inside the roadhouse. His late dinner was hardly satisfying, but he had no time to linger; there was a schedule to save.

Brushing his hands on the sides of his trousers, he swallowed the remainder of his meal and continued his watch upon the passengers.

An elderly citizens' club. Forty of them.

They had all eaten together in the roadhouse and were preparing to depart. They looked as weary as he was as they struggled through the narrow doorway of the bus, assisting each other with their walking frames and canes. Once the coach had consumed the last of them, Michael sighed and rose from the booth. His buttocks felt like they had formed sharp edges from his uncomfortable seat. Stretching his back and rubbing his eyes, he was startled by the annoying ring tone of his small mobile. Yawning as he dug it from out the depths of his rear pocket, he brought the loud device to his ear. "Yeah?"

"Michael, where are you?" asked Geoff, his boss.

"Point Cook. We've just had dinner," Michael answered on the tail of a yawn.

"What? You're joking. You were supposed to be at the Geelong Hotel, damn it! That group has bookings early tomorrow at the Bowls Club. What the hell have you been doing?"

"Settle down, will you? They are a seniors' club, not a bunch of eighteen-year-old boys on a football trip. These kinds of tours take time."

"Time? You are an hour away from Geelong, and it's past eight o'clock already!"

"I'm aware of that," Michael grumbled as he stared at his watch, feeling a great weight on his shoulders.

"I'm getting sick of this, Mick," Geoff sighed. "It's happening too often nowadays. The last three tours have been riddled with late arrivals because of *you*. Consider this your last one if I have to make excuses for you again."

Michael fell silent. He thought of his overdue rent, his divorce lawyer's fees, and his impending child support payments. He sighed and rubbed his eyes again, then opened them and watched the blur of sweat clear from his vision.

"Don't worry. I'll get them there soon," Michael said, suddenly feeling a familiar twist in the pit of his stomach.

Saturday, April 14th. The Parallel World.

"What! Who said that?" Hex yelled as he was again jolted from his sleep. He stared up at the echoing voices above him, channeling through the dark tunnels in his cave's ceiling.

He grinned and took flight.

As he flew out into the red sky, he called for his master to create another doorway. It opened a short distance away, breaking a brilliant fissure between two large clouds.

"I have him again, master!" Hex yelled. "I will return and you will think better of me!" As Hex flew he suddenly felt a sense of dread. With a gasp he entered the doorway to the mortal world, unsure of what awaited him on the other side, and vanished.

Saturday, April 14th. The Mortal World.

The highway was lonely, and the land was dark around them. The bus cruised along the cold road doing one hundred kilometers per hour. Michael's eyelids were growing heavy, so he slid open his window, hoping the cold wind would keep him awake. He eyed his passengers through his rear vision mirror. Most were asleep. One woman was fumbling through a crossword puzzle book the size of a dictionary. The man next to her, presumably her husband, was shifting uncomfortably in his seat, annoying the gentleman behind him.

Michael had a classical radio station playing softly through the front speakers. He sighed and focused back onto the dark road, watching the stretch of the coach's headlights through the late mist. He glanced at his wristwatch.

11:32 PM.

He sighed again, realizing that he was already later than he'd expected. There was supposed to be only one more hour of driving, but his passengers had taken some time to get settled before they could depart from Point Cook. A small green road sign passed on his left, indicating that he still had twenty-five kilometers to go before reaching Geelong. A shadow seemed to disturb the beams of his headlights, but only for a second. His stomach gurgled nervously.

Michael had always been haunted by a sense of foreboding. Why was he such a loser? He felt that he had been created to suffer.

Why?

Months before he was a successful supervisor. Now he was driving a bus full of old folks, and he could hardly keep his eyes open. Everything in his life had always seemed to go downhill as soon as he felt things were going well. He'd gotten so he could recognize the exact moment. He'd notice how happy he was, and immediately he'd get a sick feeling in his gut. In every case—every case!—that sensation of dread would be followed by disaster. He wondered sometimes, mostly when deep into a bottle of gin, if there were something else at play. Something in a place far out of sight and out of mind that was watching him. If there were, for some reason it had locked its sights on him and would never let go. What would make it happy? Would he need to die? Was that it? But if his death would satisfy it, why wouldn't it just be done with him?

Michael shook his head.

No, this thing wanted to torture him. Another quick disturbance of his headlight beams made him shake with alarm. His hands slipped on the wheel, and his coach swerved from side to side. He gasped and quickly straightened the large vehicle on the road. Some of his passengers noticed and started to look uneasy.

Michael's heart was pounding, and his eyes began to dart as he watched the rushing landscape. "It's out there," he thought. "It's come again. It's come to have its fun and torture me. Not tonight. Not ever!" With determination, he gripped the steering wheel and focused on the black highway ahead. "It wouldn't take much," he thought. "Just a quick spin of the wheel . . . I'd be free."

No, Michael!

What was that? Was it someone's voice in his head? An impostor? The voices and thoughts he normally heard were his own, but that one? It sounded large, profound, as if it had come from the mouth of a beast— *the* beast?

No, Michael!

There it was again, as clear as anything—did anyone else hear? He was tempted to ask his passengers, but couldn't. They'd think he was nuts!

I'm not here to torture you, Michael. I need you.

Michael searched the view outside. His gasps had become loud enough for his passengers to hear. Most had awakened. Some were becoming frightened; he was panting like a tired dog.

Please, Michael. Easy does it . . . slow the coach down.

Michael caught sight of the speedometer—one hundred and twenty kilometers per hour and climbing.

Michael, please. I will explain everything.

"What are you?" he asked with his thoughts.

I am Hex. Your Hex. I am bound to you, as you are to me. I can't exist without you, Michael. So please, stop your coach.

"You . . . you are the reason for my crappy life?"

You are not as insignificant as you think you are. You are special.

"What?"

Slow the coach down and I'll explain—

"Tell me now!" he said aloud, and suddenly there was panic amongst his passengers.

Michael, please . . .

"You've taken everything I care about away from me. Why?" Michael yelled. He didn't care about the panic he was creating around him. It seemed irrelevant. He'd suddenly discovered the beast responsible for his misfortune, and he wasn't about to let go.

Your losses were unfortunate, and I am sorry. But you are part of a greater plan. Please stop before—

"What plan?"

My world. Your world . . . they are both in danger. My interventions that lead to human deaths will help cure the earth.

MEETING YOUR HEX

"Deaths?" Michael asked, thinking back over everything that had happened to him. "The accident. The accident outside the factory? That was you? You did that?"

Yes.

"That driver had a family! He was a grandfather! A businessman died too! And a mother of three!"

They were sacrifices for the greater good. Their losses are a small price to pay in comparison to what we all could lose.

"You need people to die? Is that it?"

Yes. Please stop the coach, Michael.

"These people . . . you want these people? My passengers?"

Please stop the coach.

"You're not touching them. None of them!"

Michael eased his foot off the accelerator and brought the large bus to a stop by the side of the road. His terrified passengers were milling about the cabin.

"What are you doing?" one of them called.

"We'll call the police! You shouldn't be driving!" another yelled, almost spitting out her false teeth.

"Driving and drugs!" another accused.

"I need to get some air," Michael called back at them as he unbuckled his seat belt and stepped out.

The late chill gripped his flesh as he leaped down onto the gravel and ran into the dark.

"What are you doing, Michael?"

The deep voice seemed to be traveling around him then, as if it were flying. It had spoken out loud and not in his head this time. He kept on running. Into the dark. Into the unknown.

"Michael, stop! I can talk to you now, but you must stop."

"Leave me alone! You've done enough to me," Michael gasped as his heart struggled to keep his thick blood circulating.

"I will never kill you. I need you."

"But you will kill others."

"Not directly. Just through circumstance. Please, Michael."

Michael stopped and dropped to his knees. He leaned on a rotten wooden post, which was slanting by his side. It looked like part of a decaying fence line. As his hands dropped to the ground, his fingers hit something sharp. Working the dirt in the blackness, he discovered shards of glass. Their small points pierced his hands, and he could feel the blood oozing out. His eyes adjusted to the darkness, and he realized that he was beside an old car wreck.

Please, Michael. Just go back to the coach, and I'll leave you alone for tonight.

"You need to find someone else to taunt," Michael said as he gripped a large shard in his right hand.

There is no one else. You are my only link to the mortal earth. Others like me are more powerful than I. They can cause earthquakes and other disasters. But me? All I have is you.

"You are my bad luck?" Michael asked, weeping.

Yes. But you are my fortune, my only hope to serve my master.

"Not anymore."

When Michael plunged the shard of glass into his own throat, a roar from the air above him thundered the ground. He felt the sudden embrace of enormous arms. The beast was crying.

Crying for him.

For both of them.

Michael pillowed himself in the warmth of the creature that had caused him so much sorrow. As his blood pooled beneath them in the darkness, he felt cold.

Soon after that, after a lifetime of waiting, he felt nothing.

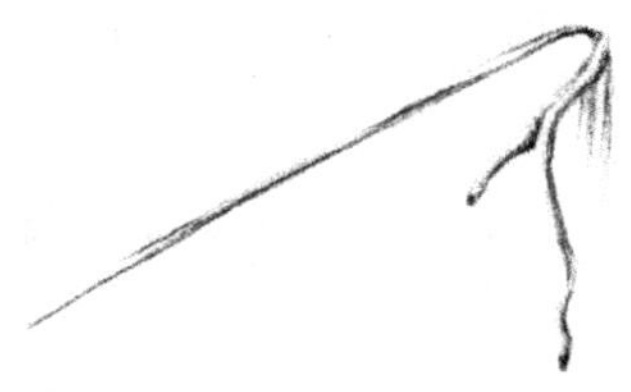

VOW'S PASSAGE

In hell, hope is an indulgence. The ultimate risk. For a bruised spirit such as Sally, the safest option might just be the devil you know. Just ask her. More likely than not, she'll tell you that in hell, hope is a mortal sin.

—Mark Farrugia, author of the *Allure of the Ancients* comic series and *Seeds*

Sally watched as the demons pulled another petrified soul from the cage. Another condemned one like her.

She looked on in terror as the damned were ripped from their places. Razor-sharp claws clasped their flesh and left behind dangling arms on the hot metal grid.

The cacophony grew, a riot of thumping drums of stretched mortal skin, strings of entrails strumming chords like haunted harps, and screaming vocals from a choir of horned singers. Out the condemned went into the demonic rave.

Out into hell.

To dance.

To be fucked.

To be torn, to be drunk from, and then to be discarded under demonic feet until reduced to steaming pulp.

Soon the cage was empty.

All but for Sally.

In snaked the hands, which grabbed and ripped at her shirt and jeans. Sally was thrown screaming out into the throng of beasts large and small, hoisted onto horns, onto muscled arms, onto hard cocks. They toyed and they laughed, throwing her to and fro until they fumbled and she fell hard to the heated stone underfoot. Her hands burned as she

THE CAGE

lifted herself to her feet. Countless clawed fingers stretched out to snatch her up again, cutting into the mortal flesh of her shoulders and arms. Her skin melted at the touch of their talons, red hot like fire. She screamed in agony and dropped to her knees, then scurried on all fours, in between parted legs, slipping on demonic filth as she struggled to gain her feet. Then somehow, as the disgusting slime thinned underfoot, it caked on her soles and she achieved traction.

Finally she could run.

Sally could see an opening within one of the great walls—walls that soared to tremendous heights.

The demons gave chase. They ran, they slithered, they flew, they galloped, and they strode, screaming, roaring, and laughing.

The dark tunnel was narrow, and she turned and twisted through its black labyrinth, diving farther and farther into the unknown. The echoes of laughter, snarls, and roars traveled through the passage, taunting her.

Suddenly she hit a large, hot gate, and it burned her mortal flesh even more. She kicked it with all her might, but the gate was impenetrable. She cried, dreading their teeth, their claws, their tongues, and their sex. Bleeding and trembling, she waited for her impending doom.

Then something gripped her ankle, and she gasped. It squeezed and it tugged from the darkness until, only seconds from capture, she was snatched from the demons. The thing dragged her into hidden depths beneath the stone wall, its fingers tight and hot. Suddenly, she was on her back, and the hold on her was released.

Whatever had claimed her ignited a blue flame that gave vision to a small, hot chamber. The thing lunged onto her, its pointed fingers gripping her throat, and she felt the tender skin beneath its grasp burn. Choking, she thrust her hands forward with all her might to push away her attacker. To her surprise, the move worked, and she was suddenly free of its burning grip. She heard it hit a hidden wall and pant painful breaths. Steeling herself, she prepared for it to advance again, but instead she heard wheezing, and then something her terrified mind did not expect.

It began to weep.

Sally trembled where she stood and listened to the struggling rustle of the sorrowful attacker. The blue flame showed its features as it labored out of the shadows. It was small and wretched—had she wounded it that badly? Its muscles were clearly defined around its scrawny frame. Tiny sharp horns protruded from the sides of its head, and a thin tail swayed lazily behind its rear.

The creature sniffled through its tears. "Y-you need not fear me. I am t-too weak to feed on you . . . my name is Vow." *Sniff. Sniff.* "What is your name?"

VOW

"S-Sally."

"You have been wounded by the demons, Sally. I can smell your blood cooking," Vow said.

Sally trembled and nodded. "What are you?" she asked as she touched her wounds with tender fingers.

"I was like you. One of the condemned. Long ago." It stepped closer as its neck twitched, its pain visible on its knotted face.

"L-like me? I-I don't understand."

The demon pointed to the wounds on her shoulders and then to the matted scars that mapped its scrawny torso. "They had their claws in me when they pulled me from the cage. I got away . . . I hid in here . . . and then I changed," it explained painfully, its tiny jaws glowing in the dark. "You will change too."

Sally rose to her feet, her eyes wild with terror.

"No!" she cried.

"You will be like me. Like them. But don't give up hope," Vow muttered. He dropped to his knees in exhaustion. Sally went to his aid. She pitied him, and she could imagine a picture of her own future. Her own doom.

"Hope?" Sally uttered as Vow fell into her arms. "There is no hope for us."

"Y-you saw the gate outside?" Vow wheezed.

"Yes."

He trembled as if his body were struggling to hold onto life. He pointed a shaking finger into the darkness. Sally's eyes followed. She could just make out the contours of a passage.

"I-I have dug around it. Around the gate. You must try, for your own sake . . . Try and finish what I have begun."

"What have you begun?"

"Th-the passage. It may lead to a way out."

"Out of here?"

"Out from hell."

Vow coughed painfully and gurgled his last words, lifting himself as close to Sally's face as he could. "Eat me. Eat my meat. You will get stronger. You will get strength from my flesh . . . Dig . . . dig . . . *escape*."

Vow fell limp in her arms, his head flopping to one side. Sally allowed him to fall at her feet. She didn't want to eat him, but she could not get his last words out of her head. He wanted her to devour him? She stared at his body and took in the smell of his death as it steamed on the hot floor.

Vow's meat already smelt of decay. The stink made her dry-retch. How could she possibly eat him?

HELL'S CHILDREN

But in the darkness of the chamber, in the silence and the heat with only the pain of her wounds to keep her company, Sally began to feel her hunger and growing weakness. She glanced to and from Vow's remains for a time, until finally, she surrendered to her hunger.

She sniffed. She picked and she nibbled.

Then, she ate him all.

Stronger now, Sally ventured into the darkness of Vow's passage until she found its end. Feeling the hot stone wall with her fingers, she could tell that Vow had burrowed through the stone with nothing but his own hands. Believing that such a task was beyond her, she clawed at the wall; the hot stone came away more easily than she'd expected. Fueled by the strength that Vow's flesh and blood had given her, she burrowed through the stone like a mole.

As she worked, she felt herself changing. First came the small horns at the top of her forehead, then came the fine dark fur over her breasts and shoulders. Even her breaths as she labored sounded more beastly, more . . . hellish. Soon her tail emerged from her lower back.

By the end of her arduous work, she was using more than just her hands to dig at the stone. She bit at it with her newly formed fangs, and kicked at it with her feet, which bore a set of talons that would suit the likes of a prehistoric meat eater. She leapt from edge to edge of the passage she'd created, pulling, digging, kicking and biting at every opportunity, until finally, she'd created an opening.

Through the fissure in her wall blew a surge of hot air, hot enough to score even her demonic flesh. She leapt back in agony but feasted her eyes nonetheless at her achievement. She cautiously broke away the stone, increasing the size of the fissure. The soaring heat that blew in from the other side became less intense as the crevice grew. The end of her passage soon gave way, and the stone collapsed to leave an entrance into a new level of hell.

Sally climbed over the piles of heated stone at the base of the doorway and took in her discovery. Before her lay a cavern of enormous proportions, a subterraneous world that was limitless to her gaze. Demonic architecture was ablaze. The sight of the stone structures, angled and crudely constructed, made Sally cringe. Homeland of the demons, flaming and stretching up towards a darkness of incredible heights. Sally felt the heat more intensely with every step. Then she caught sight of a set of stairs carved into the side of one of the enormous walls.

Without thinking about the heat that had began to blister her cheeks, she ran for them. They led up, way up, perhaps towards another doorway somewhere up in the heights. Was there a gate that showed the light of day? She could only dare to hope with every agonizing step.

With her mind fixed on exodus, Sally did not think about other possibilities. Not just that there might be a doorway to freedom, but that something terrible could be guarding it. Suddenly she felt a tug at her leg, and before she knew it, she had been plucked up and was dangling before an enormous and monstrous mouth. A tongue, larger than a tidal wave, licked the tips of jaws that were born and made of fire.

Sally looked up towards the great heights where the stairs climbed, and caught a hint of daylight flickering through the darkness.

Vow's passage did lead to a way out, she thought before the gigantic jaws closed in around her.

WAR OF ME

They say children suffer the most in wars of broken hearts; after all, our parents' blood flows through our veins. Shudder to think when one of them wants it back . . .

—Greg Chapman, author of *Torment, The Noctuary, Vaudeville,* and *The Last Night of October*

I crept out of my bedroom and found him in the same place after daybreak. He stood before our large living room window, which gave onto a view of the waking dawn. I stepped cautiously towards him, but he did not move. He was as frozen as a sculpted gargoyle. His stance was tense and his grip on the shotgun was firm and at the ready. "Papa?" I asked him quietly.

As if disturbed from a troubled sleep, he snapped his gaze to me with eyes that were wild and bloodshot. The longer he stared, the more he relaxed; he remembered who I was. Warmth returned to his face. His love did not weaken, no matter how hard the times were.

He gave me a small grin. The slightest. His eyes motioned for me to go into the kitchen, and I obeyed.

I took my seat at the table and waited. He followed a few moments later. He placed a bowl and some cereal before me and turned on the kettle. I listened to the winds outside. They were howling eerily around our lonely house. A house surrounded by miles of open land, which was orange beneath the rising sun. A house far away from everything, but so exposed to those we fear.

Our lonesome shelter in the mouth of hell.

THE LONESOME SHELTER

Papa sat at the table with his gun resting at his side. He sipped at his steaming cup and sighed. I wanted to talk to him, but there was little to say. Nothing. We just lived. I slept, and sometimes I would play as Papa's eyes would gaze out into the vacant lands, watching. He would never let me go outside. I couldn't remember the last time my feet had touched the earth, or felt dust in between my toes. Daylight was no longer safe, no matter what the books would try to have us believe. Papa had not slept for a long time. It seemed like an eternity since I had last seen him sleep.

He hadn't been able to rest since Momma was taken.

A noise interrupted our silence and Papa spilt his cup as he rose from his chair. His head turned in all directions, as if trying to lock eyes on an invisible wasp. My heart began to race. The noise traveled in the winds and swirled around our home. It gushed through our dancing curtains.

It was them . . . they were calling.

Screams from the evil ones. They sounded like tortured bats. I could picture their advance upon the house. In a line, they would march behind their leader, slowly but surely making their way to our fence lines. Their eyes were white orbs, their skin grey and lifeless, their mouths wet with thirst for our blood.

The screams grew louder, and Papa ordered me to my bedroom. I leapt out of my chair, my teddy hugged to my chest, and ran for the hall. I heard Papa's feet as they pounded from window to window. The lock-and-loading snaps of the rifles he kept at each boarded window always sent shivers through my veins.

I hid beneath my bed as usual and dressed myself in the necklaces of garlic cloves I kept there. I hugged my teddy and cried as Papa's gunshots echoed over the land. Fewer came every time, but she would not let them give up. Although vampire blood flowed through her veins, no darkness could diminish the true nature of her dead heart.

And so, Papa and Momma would have their war . . .

Their war of me.

HEARTS OF WINTER

Sanctuary, the place where we all run to feel safe. But sometimes, sanctuary isn't the safest place at all.

—Andrew J McKiernan, author of *All the Clowns in Clowntown, The Final Degustation of Doctor Ernest Blenheim* and *They Don't Know That We Know What They Know*

"Just settle now, lad. We're nearly there."

"Please, officer. I don't want you to take me back."

The officer grinned, eyeing him through the rear vision mirror, a boy reminiscent of his own son, who was always reluctant to attend Sunday services.

He parked outside the old orphanage. The headlights of his patrol car beamed through the mist, illuminating a large stone crucifix. He turned to the boy, who was shifting nervously in the shadows. "Quick now, lad. A storm is brewing."

The officer stepped out into the night, adjusting his collar to shield him from the late chill.

The boy tugged the officer's coat. "Please. Don't take me to the door," he whispered.

The officer crouched. "Don't fear, son. This is a house of the Lord." He playfully tapped the boy's head and then led him beyond the large cross and down a winding path. A murky haze shrouded their feet whilst distant thunder cracked.

An old priest was waiting for them at the front door.

"Father," the officer said, flicking the visor of his cap. "I hear this lad has done a run on you before. Perhaps you should keep him on a leash. The town's a dangerous place after dark."

FATHER WHO AREN'T IN HEAVEN

The priest smiled, winkles webbing across his face. He made way for the boy to enter. The boy looked up at the officer sadly before disappearing into the shadows of the hall.

The priest gave the officer a thankful nod, then revealed a hand beneath his robe. He was clasping an ancient carved stone dagger in his skinny fingers. Long fingernails, grown for a single purpose, ended each digit. His smile widened unnaturally.

The officer reached for his revolver, hands fumbling at the grip. The priest drove the dagger deep beneath the officer's ribs, skillfully turning and ripping through cloth and flesh. Then his fingernails went to work, carving out a passage to the warm, thudding heart.

The boy watched the ritual from within the hall. Resting in his trembling hands was an old clay pot. His fear forced him to lose control of his bladder. As the wet and warm streams of urine ran down the inner sides of his legs, he sobbed, "I even tried to warm this one."

The clay pot was filled. The officer's heart still pulsed.

The gods would be appeased this winter.

DESPAIR OF THE HUNTED

When you have a couple centuries of jaded experience beneath your belt, sparring with today's slackabout youth just isn't going to cut it. Here's one vampire who knows when it's time to raise the stakes . . .

—Kirstyn McDermott, author of *Perfections* and *Caution: Contains Small Parts*

They had me cornered.

They were a common horde, all in their college years. Each of them spat words of disgust. "Monster! Demon!" I'd heard it all before.

Their stances reflected overconfidence, which suggested that I must have been their first.

As usual, I remained silent.

Before long, they raised their rifles and handguns, and without hesitation, showered me with bullets.

I listened to their footsteps disappear before rising. By then I had already regenerated.

I leapt through one of the warehouse windows in a spray of shattering glass and confronted them. They screamed as my roar cut the air. They lit the parking lot with their gunfire, but one by one, I ripped out their throats.

I picked up one of the females with a fist full of hair and drank from her. Her blood was bland and tasteless, unsatisfying.

I thought of my home again. My desire to return had reached its peak. My small cottage was hidden away within the woodlands, which rested on lands beyond the great sea. The roads that ran through the tunnels of the forest stretched out towards the gates of Romania. It was

THE HUNTED

there that I would return to now, in hope of regaining some purpose to my immortality.

The vampire hunters in the last century were something to respect, unlike the pitiful dead that lay bleeding at my feet. Sometimes I would battle a hunter for years before finally defeating him. Drinking from their throats held a sweetness unknown in other mortals. But they were getting closer to claiming my head, and in the early 1900s I was forced to flee to the western world.

Over time I developed an awareness that there is a difference between a hunter and a slayer. The hunters engaged me, sometimes hand to hand, wielding religious objects, crossbows that fired wooden bolts, stakes made from hawthorn wood, and even pouches filled with holy water. They were eccentric extremists, mysterious folk with nerve. Hunting creatures like me was their purpose, not their pastime. But I have no respect for the slayers. They are foolish hopefuls who believe killing a vampire is as easy as shooting a paper target. They are nothing but boring blood, a disgrace to their ancestors.

Romania has changed much since my last stay here, and I am saddened to admit it, but the vampire hunter has all but vanished. In his place I find the same young hordes of gun-happy fools. And as I sit in my stone cottage, drinking from the throat of another tasteless slayer, a resolution occurs to me.

The traditions of the vampire hunter have been lost. It is time for them to be restored. I have grown tired of the slaughter of fools. I thirst for the thrills of battle once again. It was never my custom to allow my victims to live, but how else would my wish be realised? I want my enemy back, and I have no choice but to create him.

When the next horde attacks me here, I will spare one of them. I will motivate him by murdering all that he holds dear. Right before his eyes.

The lonely hunter will rise again, and here in the darkness, I will be waiting.

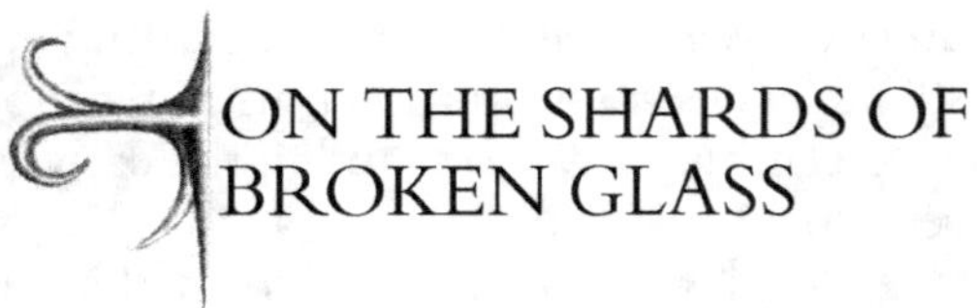 ON THE SHARDS OF BROKEN GLASS

Everyone learns from their experiences, even the worst of experiences; exactly what gets learned depends on the individual . . .

—Chuck McKenzie has previously filled the roles of genre author, editor, and reviewer, and now runs specialist bookshop *Notions Unlimited* in the eldritch seaside town of Chelsea, Victoria, where he hopes to eventually overcome his obvious allergy to money

She slipped her trembling fingers into his gloved hand and squeezed.

"Y-you don't have to do this," she sobbed.

"You're just scared. Don't worry. We know what we're doin', and we've gone too far to turn back now."

One brother turned his gaze over his shoulder and into the backseat. The other sat waiting in the darkness with two crowbars resting on his lap.

"Pass mine over," said the brother in the front. He took the metal with a firm grip and asked, "You ready?"

"Yep."

He turned back to her again and placed a hand on her shoulder.

"Stay here, and remember, you don't have to watch."

She nodded and cried as her two brothers left the car and crept off into the night.

Kerry slid his credit card off the counter and slotted it back into his leather wallet. The Asian shopkeeper bagged up his bottle of Yering Station Chardonnay and presented it to him, muttering, "Have a g-good evening, s-sir."

Kerry looked up at the shopkeeper, who appeared troubled. Was it the bruise on his forehead?

"Is everything all right? You don't look well," Kerry said, not knowing why he cared.

The shopkeeper smirked and rubbed his brow. "T-too many long hours," he mumbled. "I'd better close up."

Kerry took his bottle of liquor and tucked it beneath his overcoat. He gave the shopkeeper a small nod, buttoned up his coat, and swung open the door. Some old chimes hanging from the top of the doorway sounded. He stepped out into the chill that draped the small town of Seville.

His late model BMW was waiting in the empty parking lot. He had to squint to see the time on his gold Rolex. It was after midnight. No streets surrounded the small milk bar, only silent fields. The quiet was music to his ears. He loved that old town. Whenever the demands of his company and his wife got to be too much, he would escape there.

Three years before, he'd secretly purchased a two-bedroom cottage on the outskirts of the township. It was a tidy little hideaway. No television. No phone. A small gas cooker and an open fireplace. It was all he needed.

His life was full of endless board meetings, and his wife never seemed to stop nagging him for more money to fund the next renovation to her face. His greatest stresses, however, were the demands of his ex-mistress. He'd associated with many women over the years, and all had understood that nothing was permanent. As a consequence, he had settled most of his affairs with money, sometimes jewellery, and on one occasion, a Jaguar.

But Tracy, a young assistant, was an unstable girl, and was not letting go. For a time, he tolerated her pleas to resurrect the affair. But she'd become less discreet around his office, openly expressing her emotional torment, so in the end, he had had no choice but to fire her.

This one had really fallen for him, so buying *her* out was not an option. He didn't know what to do, but the open fireplace in the cottage would help him deal with his dilemma. He would drink the wine until nothing mattered except the flickering of the flames.

Kerry dug into his pocket for his keys and pressed the keyless entry button on the door. Two quick flashes of light from the car's indicators suddenly disturbed the darkness. His hand touched the lever, but suddenly, there was a noise.

A thudding noise.

He could hear feet running towards him. He quickly turned his gaze and saw two dark figures approaching. Each of them wielded a crowbar.

"Can I help you?" His heart began to race.

The men didn't respond and continued to close the gap. Kerry cried out; his keys dropped from his hands. As he tried to open the door, the first blow shattered his forearm. He shrieked and collapsed onto the asphalt, his newly purchased bottle of liquor smashing beneath his weight. Small shards of glass dug into his hip as the wine began to pool beneath his back.

Kerry squirmed at the throbbing pain in his arm and stared wildly up at his attackers. They towered over him, the glow of the nearby store shrouding them in shadow.

"He-help me!" he yelled, hoping the shopkeeper would call the police. "Please! Help!"

Without warning, one of the attackers bashed his weapon into Kerry's right knee. He screamed as he felt the bone break. The other attacker jabbed the curved end of his crowbar into his chest, snapping a rib. He coughed blood as he clutched at the wound in his torso. He looked up again in agony. Another crowbar was raised over his head.

He gasped when the nearest attacker halted his partner, yelling, "That's enough!" The voice sounded juvenile. The crowbar was lowered and they stood over Kerry, breathing heavily. Kerry trembled as he watched the fog of their breath steam out from the shadows of their hoods.

"Yell all you want," the one farthest away said. "You think that shopkeeper is gonna help you?"

The nearest attacker knelt slowly and said, "Gave him a visit before you arrived, so save your breath." He flicked his head, as if telling a third party to approach.

Kerry's legs shook anxiously as he heard the approaching footsteps, a clack of high heels. A woman? His agony pulsed with every beat of his heart, but an even colder chill washed over his face when the stranger came into view. She stood beside the crouched attacker, and Kerry recognised her profile instantly.

"Tra-Tracy?" he muttered painfully. The blood in his mouth was making it hard to talk.

BROKEN

She cried at the mention of her name. The standing attacker stepped towards her and placed a gentle arm around her shoulder. She accepted his comfort and cried into his chest.

"Wha-what's happening?" Kerry sobbed, watching the attacker stroke her hair, his face still draped in shadow.

The kneeling one looked up at Tracy. "Anything you wanna say to him?"

Without warning, Kerry's bladder contracted, and he soiled his trousers. The warm urine flooded over the tops of his thighs before drizzling between his legs. Tracy lifted her head and looked towards him. Her face was barely visible in the darkness, but he could make out the curves of her cheekbones. "I love you," she said.

"Please," Kerry coughed. "Wha-whatever you're telling these boys to do . . . t-tell them to stop."

"Take her back to the car," the crouched attacker said. His partner gently urged Tracy to follow him. She resisted for a few steps, but then surrendered, sheltering within his embrace as they walked away.

The crouched attacker reached into the shadows of his coat and pulled out a white hand towel. He bunched it up in his gloved hands and leaned forward. Kerry struggled as the towel neared his face, the muscles of his cheeks resisting. He could see himself being dragged off into a hidden place, his screams muffled. Chills gripped the back of his neck like an invisible hand at the thought of the final blow. Death was coming.

"Settle down, old man," the attacker said as he roughly dabbed Kerry's face. "If I wanted you dead, it would've happened already. Just calm down and listen," he said, wiping the blood off Kerry's chin. He shoved the towel into a plastic bag and tucked it back into his coat.

"She's suffered enough. You know that?"

"I-I didn't me-mean to hurt her, I—"

"Shut up!" the attacker yelled. "Listen! Not bloody talk!" He jabbed a quick fist into Kerry's broken knee. Kerry yelped and squirmed as the surge of pain spiraled from his knee to his head, like an unseen snake, biting as it climbed. "You rich bastard! You think you got it all. You think you can just have anythin' you want and then toss it away when you're done?"

Kerry quivered and kept his mouth shut.

"When we were kids, we had it different, you know? Yeah, she told us about you. Grew up in North Toorak, was it? Big house? Swishy schools? Your daddy gave you a Lexus for your first car?"

Kerry nodded.

"You don't know what it feels like to cry in your own bed and hear your older sister scream in the next room. Didn't tell you that, did she?"

the attacker huffed. "Those scars on her belly? Spotting her skin like a rash? I bet she told you they came from a burning car wreck."

Kerry remained silent.

"Nope," the attacker nodded. "Our daddy's cigar. He tortured her for years. He raped her before she was fourteen. And do you want to know somethin' else?" The attacker moved in, the bridge of his nose emerging from the blackness beneath his hood. "She suffered for us. That's right. She's one brave girl, and we look up to her for that. Once my brother and I were old enough, we fried that old bastard in the bathtub. Cold water and a hair dryer did the trick. After that, you see, Tracy took care of us. She found her feet. She put herself through school. Worked her arse off in cafés and hotels for extra cash.

"All was going sweet until she got that job assisting your sorry arse! Sure, she could afford to get herself some swishy stuff, and hell, got me and my brother a couple of iPods. But, you had to go and screw it all up."

Kerry let out a tearful breath. His head swam at this wealth of information.

"What's happened tonight is simple," the attacker said as he stood. "You broke Tracy's heart, so we broke you." He leaned over and slowly waved his crowbar. "I'm wonderin' now if you're gonna be stupid or smart when folk start askin' you stuff?"

Kerry shifted painfully on the asphalt, thinking the first call he would make, after the paramedics, would be to the police.

"Well, if you choose to flap your lips, just remember that we have a towel full of your DNA . . . got the idea from TV. I'm not as dumb as you think. We can get you into a lot of strife, old man. So don't fuck with us."

"I'm g-going to t-tell the truth." Kerry groaned fearfully as his teeth began to chatter. "I f-fell down some s-stairs."

The attacker grunted as if suggesting approval and walked away into the darkness.

The car disappeared into the night, and the stillness surrounded Kerry again. He retrieved his mobile and made his desperate call for an ambulance. As he shivered to the rhythm of his agony, he began to fret about his attractive new assistant. He thought of her long legs, her flawless face, and shook the thoughts from his head. The boys had taught him a valuable lesson. One he would apply to the women of his future.

He'd start running background checks.

# TOUCHED

Oh, Eric. What have you done? Why have you done it? And who, or what, have you done it for? Poor Eric. Sometimes the choice to do evil is no choice at all.

—Lee Battersby, author of the novels *The Corpse-Rat King* (Angry Robot, 2012) and *Marching Dead* (2012), and the collection *Through Soft Air*. He lives online at www.leebattersby.com and blogs at The Battersblog (battersblog.blogspot.com)

As he stepped back from the bed, the thunder of his heart hurt his ears. Wiping the sweat from his brow with a trembling hand, he stared down at what he had done. Tears began to fill his eyes.

"Kiana?" he muttered. "Why did I do that? What just happened?"

In an attempt to startle her back to life, he lowered a hand to her bare shoulder, but recoiled when he realised there was no use.

She was gone. He could feel the warmth that had radiated from her skin already beginning to fade.

"Three years of marriage. We were happy." The tears streamed down his face. He shook as the reality of what he had done sank in.

He could not stop staring at Kiana, motionless upon the bed, her eyes facing upward, her mouth wide open, her arms at her sides.

The pale glow of the moonlight streaming in through the white bedroom drapes lit her cold face, and Eric wept into his hands.

THE DISTORTED FACE

After an eternity, he slowly lowered his hands from his face and stared at his spread fingers. The fingers that had tapped calculations into payroll software for five years. The fingers that would glide gently over Kiana's face whenever she told him how much she loved him. The fingers that had gripped her throat and squeezed the life out of her. His knees began to shake beneath his weight, and his breathing grew heavier as the seconds ticked by.

Suddenly he could feel a strange presence behind him. It *spoke*.

"So, it is done," a voice said softly.

Eric turned to the voice that came from the doorway but couldn't make out the stranger's face. Even when the man stepped in, brushing casually past Eric and walking to the window side of the bed, the glow from the moonlight silhouetted him, and it was impossible for Eric to see his face.

"Who the hell are you?" Eric asked through his tears, feeling the massive lump that had grown in his throat.

"I forgive you, Eric. I don't expect you to remember me," said the man.

There was an odd familiarity to the stranger's voice that puzzled Eric. He tried to remember where he had heard the voice before. It sounded like it was coming from someone middle-aged, yet he felt something odd beneath the words—something . . . old.

He thought about what he'd done that day. *The bus stop? The man at the bus stop? The one with the magazine? He sat next to me. Spoke to me briefly.*

"That's right, Eric. You *do* remember," said the man.

Eric felt a chill run up his back as he realised that his mind had just been read.

"What the hell are you?"

"Something that has followed you for some time," Jason replied before turning his head towards Kiana. "Something that followed her," he continued in a whisper.

"What?" Eric muttered, ready to collapse.

"Don't worry, Eric. You were only doing what I commanded you to do," Jason said.

"You made me do this?" Eric's tears intensified and began to affect his breathing.

"When I touched you. This morning. A single fingertip on your hand was enough for me to infiltrate your mind. To bend you to my will. All has happened this evening according to my desire."

"Why?" Eric cried.

"I have searched many years for a vessel, Eric. I am the keeper of another soul that needs one. A new body. A dominion for my lost love. I had almost given up—until the day I first saw your wife. Her walk. The way she held herself. She is perfect. Just like . . . " A glossy shine began to develop in Jason's eyes, as if he were about to shed his own tears. "She will do nicely."

"Why did you make me kill her?" Eric yelled.

Jason sighed. "I am many things, Eric, but there are some deeds I just cannot carry out. That's why I need people like you . . . and things like him."

Eric felt yet another presence behind him and turned to face it. Appearing in the doorway was another dark figure. It entered the room slowly, with light steps, giving the impression that if it were to run, it could do so at an enormous speed.

When he realised that what had entered the room was far from human, the hairs on the back of Eric's neck stood to attention. The thing was standing in the moonlight, gazing back at him eagerly. His eyes twitched as he stared into a ghastly, distorted face.

The thing's eyes were unaligned, sunken, and shadowed completely by the overhang of its fleshy brow, its nose but a pair of seeping nostrils smeared downwards, following the patterned sagging of its deep wrinkles. The ears, which dominated the outline of its head, were huge, thinly skinned and veined, covering each side of the skull and pointing outward. The mouth, from which came a wheezing inhale and exhale, spread across the thing's face. Its lips were thin and dark, piercing through the gloom with a sickly grin. Its jagged teeth overlapped each other in a tangle of pointing spikes and dripped with thick and stringy saliva.

The horrendous creature inched toward Eric, who instinctively stepped back, lifting his arms defensively.

"Please don't fight it, Eric," said Jason. "I promise you, it will be quick."

SOULLESS

When a pal's feeling down, what's there to do but take them out for the night? Even if, like young Sheldon here, they don't much want to go.

—Jason Nahrung, author of *The Darkness Within* (Hachette Australia), *Salvage* (Twelfth Planet Press) and *Blood and Dust* (Xoum)

Dyson didn't wait for an invitation; he never did. He simply stepped through the door of Sheldon's apartment almost as soon as it had opened. He could feel Sheldon grimace at him as he did so, but he didn't care. He strode into the gloom of the man's privacy as if he owned it, and immediately started poking his nose into all that surrounded him. Before Sheldon had closed the door, Dyson had already voiced his distaste at the state of the place; Sheldon lived like a pig.

Dyson stepped over the piles of dirty laundry and began to randomly pick items off Sheldon's cluttered shelves, peering at them curiously. Old photographs, bubble domes, collectors' spoons, and books he'd never heard of.

"Boy, you don't get out much, loser."

Sheldon intervened promptly, snatching his private possessions and placing them back neatly. Dyson laughed, knowing that his behavior was having the desired effect. He'd had enough of *that* fun, and then proceeded to kick at the clothes that littered the floor.

"Stop that!"

"I don't suppose you have anything clean amongst this lot?"

"This isn't a good time—"

"Isn't it? It hasn't been a good time for two weeks! I've come to take you out of here!" Dyson said excitedly. "Come on! Dig your hands into your sty and find something to put on. We're going out!"

"I'm not in the mood!"

"Bullshi—"

Dyson stopped as he noticed the glare of Sheldon's computer screen from across the room and quickly pranced over to it; he was not finished yet.

"Get away from there. That's private!"

"Well, well, well! What have we got here?" teased Dyson as he arched over the keyboard. "A chat room, is it? Who are you planning on screwing?"

"Get out of there!" Sheldon snapped as he shoved him aside and switched off the monitor.

"All right, all right, lover boy!" Dyson laughed, easing back with open hands. "I'm just having fun."

"You mean being an ass!"

"Yeah! That's me, right? Come on, get dressed!"

"No."

"Yes!"

"I want to be alone!"

"You've had enough of that. It's time to go out and—"

"No!" Sheldon yelled.

Dyson stood silent. Sheldon was usually well mannered, and a pushover most of the time, so the sudden outburst was unexpected.

"Look . . ." Sheldon began, sighing and rubbing his brow. "I know what you're trying to do, and I appreciate it. Really. But I just want to be alone."

Dyson remained quiet for a few moments; that was a big deal for him. What's more, he was speaking seriously, which he did rarely.

"I know what you're going through, ya know? That's why I'm here. The first time is always the hardest, but in your case, it's been a few times now, and you're still not handling it. Sheldon, come on. Our boss is getting pissed. He spent a lot of cash getting you trained, and when you slack off like this, that makes for one unhappy millionaire."

"Maybe I'm just not cut out for this," Sheldon sighed. "How do you do it?"

"It's the job. I remember when I first put a hole in some loser's head. I did what you are doing now. I hid from everyone and watched countless videos and lived like a bum. I thought that feeling sorry for myself would help, but it didn't. I know, Sheldon."

"I still don't—"

"Look, I know I'm an ass, and the last person you want to be around. But I know what you are going through, and as much of a prick as I am most of the time, right now I care. Now go and get into something reasonable!"

"If I come, will you start treating me like a human being?"

"Not a chance," Dyson smirked.

"I'll see what I can find," Sheldon said, with a hint of a smile.

Dyson watched as Sheldon turned and disappeared into the murk of his bedroom.

"It does get easier, ya know. In the end, they're just a fleshy target," Dyson called out encouragingly as he waited in the living room.

"You're not taking me to anyplace sleazy, are you?" Sheldon called back, sounding as if he was pulling a shirt over his head.

"That's a matter of opinion."

When Sheldon finally emerged wearing an ensemble barely fit for a junkie, he paused.

Dyson skillfully pulled out his silenced .45 and fired three slugs into Sheldon's chest. He stepped over him as the gun barrel smoked and planted two more bullets into his temple.

Dyson spat down at Sheldon's corpse and muttered, "Loser."

He tucked away the tool of his trade and straightened his coat.

He went back out into the bustle of the city as his fingers jostled notes within his pockets—notes detailing names and locations.

It was going to be a long night.

BEASTS OF THE DANUBE DELTA

Postcard fiction in the Romanian wilderness as Luther and his family encounter the native population. What David Schembri offers us here is the disparity of twin monsters . . . and the chosen victor revealed by moonlight.

—Matthew Tait, author of *Dark Meridian* and writer/critic for *Hellnotes*

After a long and arduous journey, Luther and his family found themselves in an old Romanian wilderness area nestled between the Sulina and Chilia branches of the Danube delta. There the trees, which seemed too large for comfort, stretched out towards the stars, their limbs woven with thick ivy. Their aromas—pine, oak, lime, and elm—filled the icy air, and their foliage, fallen from the narrow-leafed ash trees, draped the ground underfoot.

Luther ran with his family in tow and adjusted his eyes to the dense twilight, mapping the path ahead through the thicket. Suddenly, he heard a loud rustling from the woodlands and snapped his gaze to what seemed to be the source. Howls filled the wild in varying pitches and tones, making it difficult for Luther to estimate their numbers. He clasped his bride's cold hand (her beauty was like a glowing ember) and hushed his two children (a boy and girl) as they began to ask about this choral session. Luther sniffed vigorously in the midnight chill like a wildcat and whispered, "The beasts of this realm are hunting."

He sniffed again.

"They have sensed our presence . . . they are rallying towards us."

BEASTS OF THE REALM

He hurried his family through the murk, their breaths rapid as they brushed the dangling vines. The foliage of the dense forest shrubs (typically yellow in autumn) glowed white in the moonlight. When the four of them had reached a clearing that was filled with meter-high dwarf cherry, Luther urged his family into the hardy growth and huddled them close. They watched together, the children's little bodies trembling with cold; they were accustomed to hotter climates.

As the gray wolves emerged from the thick of the surrounding woodlands, the family could see their white, glowing eyes. Inching closer, the beasts growled and surrounded the trembling feast. They were a large pack, nearly a dozen. They snarled, incisors bared, backs arched, fur bristled, and in the gloom they circled the trespassers.

Luther released his hold on his family, and as a howling wind surged, discharging a flock of crows from the treetops, the gray wolves crouched and attacked.

Jaws dug into flesh, joints were pulled from joints, veins and arteries were ripped from their places, and blood that was once warm cooled in the night.

Within moments, silence had returned to the clearing, and Luther went to work, stripping the wolf carcasses of their fur; they would later be sewn into coats. His children, tired of collecting the dead for their father, picked at the deciduous, cherry-bearing shrubs and sucked at their juices. His bride gathered wood to build a fire and provide a small taste of their true home.

The gray wolves of the Danube delta were deadly and cunning, but they were no match for the demons.

PARHELION:
Rage of the Starborn

Mankind's future resides in space; this is no surprise. But in this thrilling space adventure, Dave reveals that the wild new space nation born of idealism hasn't lived up to its promise. Now Parhelion must look to an assassin, of all people, to rediscover its humanity—if he can survive. Because in Parhelion, there is always someone who wants someone else dead.

—Marty Young, a Bram Stoker-nominated and Australian Shadows-award-winning editor, fiction, and nonfiction writer, and sometimes ghost hunter. He's mostly nuts, though

www.martyyoung.com

MYLES

Introduction

It was less than a century ago that man linked three space stations together. An enormous loop of distant lights, like the bright spots on either side of the sun, spreading its ring around the glowing Earth. It was a new orbiting world enriched with the hopes of further exploration, from the moon to our distant neighbors. But something unexpected compromised those dreams.

Non-government corporations had increasingly acquired space real estate, devouring more and more resources. This cycle continued for years as industries and technologies advanced. Longer stays upon the stations had become possible and full livability followed. What was supposed to have been an incubator for research and discovery had evolved into another breeding ground for humans. To pollute and to corrupt.

Shortly before 2252, the stations had produced their first group of children, humans not born of the earth, but of space. They were known as the starborn, and they had pale skin and eyes. With them came the realization that the stations had developed into something more than just business parks in space; they had become humanity's future. And so after the dawn of 2254, the station ring got its own government. A new nation was recognised and crowned Parhelion.

PART 1
The Awakening

Jeshan is an effective killer. Professional. Precise. He used to be the trusted executioner of crime overlord Carl Baxter. The Baxter family has its fingers in every corner of the orbiting nation and most countries on earth. Jeshan himself is a blood relation, although distant, and he is still considered one of the untouchables—one of the family.

When Parhelion was first established, the "respected" members of the weak central government were easy to bribe and blackmail, and the Baxter family was able to establish symbiotic relationships with legitimate businesses. Carl was quick to capitalize on newly opened markets in Parhelion, and his empire grew.

Carl Baxter was indeed a mobster, but at the same time, he was also a visionary. Although he used illegal means to gain profits, he *cared* about the future of Parhelion. His dreams and those of the creators were the same, and he wanted to insure a bright future for exploration. You could say that's why it was so easy for Carl to get the government to do his bidding. The stories each told were the same.

But things had changed.

It was only a year ago that Carl Baxter was reported dead, and now his wild and unpredictable starborn son heads his empire. Everyone who inhabits the station ring knows of Myles Baxter and wishes they didn't.

The passing of the crime father in a suspicious cruiser accident left this lunatic in charge of an empire that is too large for him to handle. Myles Baxter doesn't understand how to manage it, and for the most part, doesn't care. He takes pleasure in creating misery. What was a developing and controlled organisation has fallen into chaos and bloodshed.

Myles Baxter hands out death notices faster than you can blink, exterminating anyone threatening his position. "A psychopath at the helm of power," Jeshan labels him. His victims have devolved from high-profile targets to good people who have simply made the wrong choices and are easily corrupted. It won't be long before Parhelion is transformed into a slum, where no one is safe and the station ring will not see its true destiny.

On this night Jeshan is to visit a house in the eastern sector. A visit that will change the course of things as he knows them.

Jeshan hotwires the blast doors to open just after 10:00 PM. With his blaster at the ready he stands before the gloom of the interior. The place is still, as if it's vacant. Paper and garbage litter the floor, and the open kitchen area looks to be growing its own form of fungus within a mountain of unwashed dishes. Jeshan hears a noise and tenses. Sounds of thumping and struggling are coming from one of the rooms. He walks towards the door and slides it open quietly.

The occupants are unaware of his presence, giving him the opportunity to witness the goings-on. Jeshan has never seen such acts and blinks his starborn eyes to make sure they're not deceiving him. He has been ordered to neutralize three targets. A family. A father and his son and daughter. He did not expect one of them to be a child.

The father and son, Hank and Scud (detailed in the contract), are beating on the daughter—Arial, as she is identified in the documentation. She looks about seven. Hank and Scud are yelling at her as they bash their fists into her small body and fling their open hands across her face.

"Where did you hide it?" Hank yells.

"You sneaky little bitch!" Scud screams.

Arial says nothing. She just cries. Jeshan can see that Hank is holding a smoking cigar in one hand. He has one of Arial's trembling legs gripped with the other and is using it to burn a trail of red and brown spots into her flesh.

Enough. Jeshan cannot handle the sight a second longer. Time to complete the assignment. He steps into the room to ensure an optimum range and aims his blaster. Hank and Scud notice him and turn to their executioner. There is a slight pause, but the men are lost for words; they know what Jeshan is there to do. To all of them.

"S-she has the stuff!" Scud says.

"Tell Baxter he can have her as compensation. We can cut a deal," says Hank.

Jeshan lets his blaster do the answering and takes them both out with shots to each of their foreheads. Arial screams as she's sprayed with blood and brain matter. Jeshan knows that he is supposed to fire once more, yet he pauses. Arial is trembling on the bed; she stares at him through the gloom. Her breaths pulse with the rhythm of not only fear, but pain. The burns, perhaps, or . . . She squirms and cringes too. Something else is wrong with her. Something he can't see, at least in such dark lighting.

What does it matter? his mind argues. Complete the contract. We are here to kill, not investigate. Jeshan looks at the girl in misery on the bed. At least the blaster will ease the suffering.

He's killed many females in his career. It's usually been a case of them being in the wrong place at the wrong time. Sex workers, girlfriends, even relations. It was always such a waste. But this collateral damage goes with the territory.

Yet this is not an adult who has made the wrong choice. This is a young girl—a child.

Jeshan can even see a teddy bear tangled in the sheets by her feet.

WHEN LIFE WAS NOT TAKEN

This he's not encountered before. His heart has begun to race and he can't understand why. A chill rises from his flesh and puts him in an uncomfortable sweat. *Kill her? For Baxter? For that scumbag?*

"Help me," Arial whimpers in a voice that's nearly too soft for Jeshan to hear.

For a moment, Jeshan is frozen.

He steps to the bedside, instinctively still aiming his weapon. He activates a small torch that is fixed to his firearm and it drapes her in a pale white glow. The improved lighting gives Jeshan a cruel visual of the state of her face. Blood pools over her lips and streams out of her nose. Her eyes are black with bruises, and some of her long dark hair looks to have been pulled off her scalp. She is a being of the earth. He can tell because her eyes are dark; starborn children have no colour to their eyes, just a pale gray.

He kneels down and extends a hand to her. She flinches but he continues to examine, gently palpating her head for fractures and her wrists for breakages. He settles his fingers on her left elbow. Arial yelps when he applies pressure.

"The bastards broke your arm," he mutters.

Arial cries and continues to utter the words "Help me" in between her breaths.

Her large eyes transfix him. He stares into them as if hypnotized. He feels himself diving into them in spirit. Into a vast mass of ocean, into its depths, and once he's returned to the surface, something is different. He lowers his weapon and drops his head in submission.

For the first time in his life, he can't pull the trigger.

It has taken him quite some time to think of what to do. His mind, the mind of an assassin, is suddenly contemplating ideas it has not been educated to handle. He sits and stares out a window that overlooks the flying traffic of the busy eastern sector. He's cleared the sofa in the main room of the apartment and has carried Arial out and away from the corpses. He's laid her down and placed a wet cloth on her forehead, which has done nothing to ease her discomfort. He knows she requires medical attention, as her arm looks broken in more than one place. He can't take her to a care unit himself; he is an assassin and he is dressed like one. If she is to be taken to such a facility, someone else will have to drive her—but who?

The shuttle station suddenly comes to mind. There he can at least make a call for an emergency vehicle and have her collected. The health system will take it from there. They will discover she is without a family and place her in foster care.

He gathers up the child and carries her to his cruiser.

Jeshan halts after he steps through the sliding doors of the empty terminal. He narrows his eyes and takes in the quiet state of the place. Something is wrong; a shuttle station is never left unmanned.

He carries Arial to the vacant counter and places her beneath it as gently as he can. "I need to check on something. Try and be quiet," he says.

Arial nods and bites at her lip, seemingly trying to hold back her pain.

Jeshan descends into the offices nearby. Two rooms in, he hears sounds of a struggle. Through a window in an inner door, he is able to inspect the violence within. A woman is surrounded by three men. They are taunting and shoving her to and fro. With every push, their hungry hands tear at her upper garments, baring her breasts. Jeshan goes for the door as one of the men strikes her with a hard blow to the jaw. He bursts in and the startled men stare, outraged. Jeshan fires his blaster, accurately as always, and the three of them drop to the floor, now missing a face or a large portion of skull. Jeshan stands with his blaster smoking. The woman, partially covered in fragments of brain matter, gathers her torn garments to conceal her bare flesh. She is whimpering in a mix of fear, pain, and disbelief. Jeshan can tell from the look and colour of her ripped attire that she is the station master. She is slender, her hair long and dark, her eyes starborn pale, and her lips thin.

"What's your name, lady?" he asks.

She takes a few panting moments to answer.

"A-Alice."

"Clean yourself up, Alice. I need your help."

Jeshan walks Alice to the counter and reveals the child who hides beneath it. As if fueled by instinct, Alice stoops down to her. She strokes the child's face with concern. "What did you do to this girl?"

"I saved her from a wicked family. She is badly injured. If I leave her with you, can you take her to a medical facility?"

"Of course,"

"Good. Do you have a transport?"

Alice nods.

"Then let's get you both to it. Now."

Alice secures Arial into the back seat of her small cruiser, which looks to be held together with spit.

"There should've been a guard here to protect you," Jeshan says to Alice.

"One of them *was* the guard."

"Has this happened before?"

"Yes. Who are *you*?"

"Someone you may need to help in future."

She looks at him oddly, as if trying to ascertain what he's just said.

"For a young girl like you, this is a dangerous post," he says before handing her a code card. "If bandits visit you again, call me. Never hesitate."

"You'll protect me?"

"Only if you help me. Fair's fair. Right, Alice?"

She nods.

As Jeshan motions to leave, she says, "Hang on. You're not just a thug, are you?"

He faces her again.

"I mean, the way you shot those men . . . you're a pro, right?"

"What's your point?"

"Well, since when does a guy like you decide to civilize the universe?"

"Since I woke up tonight. I've been asleep for far too long."

The flight to the Baxter Plaza in the north sector is swift. Every star appears to zoom past Jeshan's craft too quickly for comfort. Every passing second reveals new territory, and this state of affairs rouses an unfamiliar emotion—fear? Jeshan keeps repeating his story in his head, even when he is standing before the new crime lord.

Myles is positioned in his usual place on his large sofa, a cigar in one hand, and a glass of whiskey in the other. The lighting is faint in the Baxter penthouse. A few scattered LED lights glow in orange cones about the enormous living area, but aside from that, all other places are dark.

One of Myles's bodyguards allows Jeshan entry onto the marble tiles. Another one of Myles's men is standing near the sofa. Myles keeps himself well guarded.

Jeshan approaches the sofa but stops as the guard nearby raises a hand to halt him. Jeshan stares at the drunk and drugged crime lord and awaits eye contact. After an endless silence, Myles looks at him with a slight smirk and eyes that drift in different directions.

"Hello, uncle," Myles mumbles.

"I'm not your uncle."

"Ah, but you are family. Blood. That's why I am keeping you around." Myles leans forward, which appears to take great effort. "And I can call you what I fucking like."

"I am your uncle then."

"You see? That's better. You are alive like a few others because I allow you to be. The family needs to exist. I believe that. My father always spoke highly of you. So, tell me, did you do what I ordered?" he says before taking in a deep drag of his cigar.

"Of course."

"Dead? Really? All three?"

Jeshan swallows before answering. "Yes. Isn't that what you wanted?"

"I would've appreciated a few souvenirs. Some fingers maybe?"

"That's not my job."

"Your job is what I dictate!"

"One of them was a child. Were you aware?"

Myles shrugs as if it doesn't matter.

"I know you hate me. Don't you, uncle?"

"So?"

"I'm not complaining. I like hate. Hate is very close to love, as they share the same level of passion."

"I don't love."

"Oh, but I do. I run them both together. Tell me, did that little girl scream when you killed her?"

"I never notice. I don't kill for pleasure."

Myles rests back into the sofa and takes another drag from his cigar. He blows it out in a stream of white smoke over his head and says, "That's a shame. You have this power to kill and get away with it, yet you don't exploit it?"

"Those are dangerous words, Myles,"

"I can afford to be dangerous, just like you can. But no, you are safe and professional like my father was. It's boring and not how I operate. People that wrong me need to suffer first."

"That little girl did nothing to you."

"She was the seed of the fuck who stole from me. That's enough for her to suffer."

"Death isn't enough for you?"

"Death should be a gift, uncle. Only granted after enough blood has been extracted."

"I am not a mutilator."

"No? If you refuse to do what I demand, then that would be unacceptable."

"Then what are you going to do? Fire me?"

"Worse. I'm demoting you."

"To do what?"

"You will be my cleaner. Just have your phone handy. I will be calling you, and when I do, you will do what I want."

Jeshan can't imagine what Myles means.

Months have passed since that night. Jeshan is looking upon life with a new perspective, a new purpose. However, his demotion has only fanned his desire to pursue what is to follow this evening.

Myles smirks and gestures his head in the direction of the penthouse bathrooms. It is 2:00 AM, the usual time Jeshan is needed to clean up. He makes his way in the dark. He is disgusted but not surprised by Myles's behaviors. He remembers stories of the crime lord as a boy, drowning his pets and making obscene gestures to the older women of the family. Jeshan only heard of such things—these were conversations not meant for his young ears—but he's filed them away in his memory. Now, the horrors that were only stories are being played out before him in full colour.

Jeshan senses one of Myles's guards following him, but he doesn't care. He flicks the switch to the bathroom and looks into a red room that would normally be white.

"Shit," he breathes. The scenes are getting worse.

"Clean this up and be out of here within the hour," orders the guard from behind.

"An hour? You kidding me? Look at this girl. She's all over the room!"

"That's your problem. Shut up and do your job."

The guard leaves the doorway and Jeshan mutters, "This isn't my fucking job, asshole."

Jeshan steps into a scene screaming with smeared blood and the smell of lead. The large spa's jets are still bubbling and Myles's latest toy is floating face down. Jeshan places his kit beside the tub and turns off the jet cycle, bringing the red water to a settling ripple. The girl's pale skin floats lazily to the edge. He turns her naked body over.

Her face is devastated, any beauty she may have possessed lost. Bite marks litter the flesh of her chest like a rash. The tile walls are splattered with blood. Jeshan can imagine the girl being flung into them, which could explain the state of her face. Blood clouds heavily between her legs, and Jeshan imagines that Myles has used implements to violate her.

Jeshan checks his watch and then turns his attention to his kit. He extracts a small unit, no bigger than the average bucket, yet it is made of some alloy. It houses a small disintegration chamber. He unclips a small laser gun from its side and turns the unit on. It hums as its engine spins. Jeshan starts with the girl's left arm. Using the laser gun like an incisor, he focuses the laser point at her shoulder and draws a line. The arm comes away as if he were tearing wet paper.

Jeshan feeds the cold limb into the small unit and it disappears, its particles taking their place in the oblivion that has engulfed so many others.

After he's cleaned the bathroom, Jeshan proceeds directly towards Myles, who sits upon his sofa throne, along with his cigar, whisky and cocaine. A guard steps in his path. "The boss has nothing to say to you. Just leave," the guard says, gripping his shoulder.

"I've got something to say to him," Jeshan retorts, staring daggers at the guard. The man is big, but he's young and unsure of himself and instantly removes his hand and steps out of the way.

"What do you want?" calls Myles from the sofa.

"What did that girl do to you? Refuse to suck your dick?"

"Why do you care, uncle?"

"Just want to know why she deserved to suffer." Jeshan shrugs. "Isn't that your motto?"

"She was a whore. She doesn't deserve pity."

Jeshan sighs. "I'm done. You can find another mortician. Don't ever call me again."

"What the fuck?"

"You heard me."

The guards look at each other in disbelief. They've never heard anyone speak such words to Myles.

"You don't have a fuckin' choice!"

"I do now, and I'm making it. Never contact me—ever."

Jeshan drops his kit and makes his exit. He is halfway down the corridor when he hears Myles yell, "What are you afraid of? Get that motherfucker back in here!"

Jeshan makes the elevator before the guards can catch up and begins the long descent to ground level. He knows that the five guards Myles has posted in the foyer of the plaza will have been alerted, so he readies himself. Ever since Myles has gained power, Jeshan hasn't been permitted to be armed when entering the plaza. No matter. He pulls himself up skillfully through the emergency manhole in the elevator's roof and waits.

The chime rings at ground level and Jeshan watches the doors open. The elevator is showered with blaster fire. Sparks and smoke shoot up through the manhole, forcing Jeshan to guard his face. When the smoke clears, he can hear the guards express confusion. Who do they think they are dealing with?

The first guard inspects the elevator, and Jeshan reaches down and hoists the man up high enough to snap his neck and snatch his weapon. Jeshan drops down using the corpse as a shield and fires precisely, killing three of the guards in quick succession. The final guard takes cover behind the chrome reception desk.

Jeshan concentrates heavy fire as he runs out. He heads for the landing platform where his cruiser waits. He hears the guard giving chase. Jeshan heads down the ramp to his vehicle, side-lit by blue lamps in the dark. He presses a button on his wrist remote and the entrance door opens before him.

He leaps on board and is soaring into space before the guard has had time to look up.

Jeshan takes the risk and goes back to his apartment. He guesses he'll make it there before any of Myles's men. At home, he has all he needs to defend himself. He arms up with his blastproof vest, daggers, toxin needles, and blaster.

It takes them an hour to melt down his door. Myles is no general, so his men have no plan. No added artillery. No Droids . . . just their numbers. Jeshan barricades himself in the rear of the apartment, transforming his kitchen into a makeshift bunker. Even though they are inexperienced gunslingers, he must not underestimate them. Doing so can result in death, even for an assassin. All he wants to do is leave one alive.

The firefight lasts for no more than a few minutes. Jeshan uses gas at first, then a smoke charger, which leaves the party in a state of utter chaos. He puts on his smoke mask, which is equipped with high-powered lenses able to see through the harshest of environments, and makes his attack. He neutralizes nine of them, his precision leaving them headless. He bashes the survivor to the ground and kicks away his weapon.

Jeshan gathers a handful of the guard's shirt and lifts him to his feet.

"P-please don't kill me," the guard begs.

Jeshan drags him out before the gas has the chance to melt the guard's lungs. He drops him on a chair in the entrance hall. "Shut the fuck up!" Jeshan yells.

He stands before the panting and petrified guard, staring, and removes his mask.

Jeshan gets out one of his small, gleaming daggers from the strap across his chest. The guard squirms. Jeshan brings the blade to his own left hand, takes a breath, and cuts off his little finger. He grunts at the sharp pain, and quickly conceals his spurting wound with a small cloth he digs out of his pocket.

He drops his finger into the guard's lap. The guard looks up at him, bewildered and horrified.

"Take that to Baxter. He likes souvenirs," Jeshan begins. "Tell him you killed me. Tell him I suffered."

Jeshan steps closer to the guard. "If you decide to fuck me, then rest assured that I will find you. I will string you up by the ankles and peel your skin down from the waste like a banana. I wonder how long it will take for you to suffocate inside your own flesh?"

The guard wets his trousers.

"Do we have a deal?"

The guard nods.

Jeshan walks to the door, collecting a small pack on his way. He takes a remote out of one of the pouches in his belt and presses a button.

"I'd get the hell out of here if I were you. This place is gonna blow."

PART 2
Man and Droid

The murk in the apartment thickens. Less traffic passes by their window at this hour, which in Parhelion time is late in the evening.

"Exclamation . . . Disgust. Anger. Annoyance," the Droid says in its low-pitched electronic voice.

Jeshan adjusts the strap on his leg holster. He has lived in the south of Parhelion for four months now. He left the name Jeshan behind him in the north. After blowing the top of his old apartment tower, he is believed dead by the Baxter empire. He has altered his appearance slightly by reducing his dark, long hair to a shadow over his scalp. He has little in the way of funds and is living from hit to hit. Those who are aware of his services in the south know him only as Conroy.

He answers the Droid. "So, in simple terms, you are in the shits."

The Droid cocks its head, analyzing the unfamiliar word with its processor. There is much ticking and spinning. A metal finger taps at the robot's rusting chin. Jeshan checks his blaster, ensuring that its sights are clean, and holsters it.

"Power?" The Droid asks for the tenth time that evening. "Need . . . power . . ." It dangles its outlet cord before its face.

"Sorry, my friend. No power."

Jeshan sighs as he rises from his couch. "I have a job tonight. Let's hope it goes well and I can pay the credits to the station lord. Then you will have your power, and I'll be able to heat my food."

"Food?"

Tick. Spin. Tick. Spin.

"That's okay. You don't have to remember why I need food."

Jeshan walks over to a small metal table and gathers his pilot card. He eyes his Droid. Its metal finger is still tapping. He grins.

The glow of the moonlight shows the Droid's contours. He has named it Decroid. After acquiring his new apartment, Jeshan went exploring and stumbled upon its remains by a facility out past the southern sector. He was surprised to find that Decroid's head casing, limbs, and torso were still intact. It seemed a waste to leave it as rubble. Decroid may have been dated technology, but Jeshan could see its potential. He had always been good with his hands. Having been born on the station ring, he found that living amongst machines was second nature. He had spent two months reassembling Decroid, which turned out to be his only company. It was low on energy and as forgetful as a space hound.

A garbage container craft slowly hovers past their window. Full visibility is restored to the room temporarily, enabling Jeshan to locate his boots. Once the lights of the large craft pass from view, the dimness shrouds them again. "I won't be long, Decroid. I should have the power back soon, providing that there are no . . . exceptions."

Tick, tick. Spin, spin.

"Except . . . shun?"

Jeshan rolls his eyes. "Never mind."

He walks to the blast doors, and his fingers search for the exit button in the shadows. The doors open and steam clouds at his feet. As the doors close behind him, he enters the elevator, which reeks of urine, and descends down towards the hanger.

Jeshan's cruiser is an old model, but efficient enough. He has had to leave his previous and more proficient craft back in the north of the station. He purchased this transport with most of what was left of his credits. Housed in its midsection is a twin turbine jet engine. At full thrust, it can orbit the earth in less than thirty minutes, which impresses him.

Exiting the hangar, he speeds out and up into the sea of flying vessels and maneuvers skillfully into the flow. He speeds through the traffic for a time before following the off lights into the deeper parts of the southern sector.

He lands on a round platform, far away from any common landing area, and turns off the lights. Hopping out, he gets his bearings and makes his way towards the sector's main strip. The south of the ring is a lower class than the rest—cheaper for the Earthborn to rent living space, and farther away from the richer parts of Parhelion to which he is more accustomed.

Scanning the busy main strip as cruisers and spacecraft speed by, Jeshan catches sight of the appointed tower, an older apartment high rise. He rushes through the bustle of late commuters as they brave the environment. Drifting bodies hover here and there among the living. Some of them will have fallen to disease. Others to asphyxiation as a result of the poor air quality within the sector's dome. However, in most cases, the bodies are a direct result of the crime wave. Flybys are common in the south, and the localized government is too weak to keep the overrun sector clean. The floating bodies are testament to the anarchy in the station ring.

Jeshan enters the tower's lobby, hurries past some loitering beggars, and leaps into an elevator. He hits the button that takes him to the one hundred and seventh floor.

MR BRANDY

The blast doors to Apartment 1102 are old and in dire need of maintenance. Rust eats away at their pistons. Jeshan frowns at the stench, a smell reminiscent of rotten cheese. The cooling systems are dated, and the air quality is barely acceptable. At least *his* apartment tower in the upper south is equipped with a nifty generator; that's why he strives to pay his rent before anything else.

He straightens his coat and presses the buzzer. A small screen protrudes from the doorframe, displaying a green, fuzzy image of the occupant, Nile Brandy. He looks more aged than Jeshan expects. The photo his client has given him is out of date. It shows Mr. Brandy in his better days. He was a high-flying property manager in his time, but all went sour when he decided to start stealing from his business partners. He's now holding onto life by a few fine threads.

Jeshan knows he can keep doing what he does best, because in Parhelion, there is always someone who wants someone else dead.

"What do you want?" Nile barks through the aging speaker.

"The name is Jennings, sir," Jeshan lies. "I'm part of the maintenance crew. I'm here to replace a card in your com unit."

"What? I wasn't told of this."

"It's routine, sir. It should only take a few minutes."

"Screw it! The com unit is fine."

"Sorry, sir. I'm under orders from management. Open the door."

"Bullshit! The manager can come here himself."

Jeshan displays a fake master key card in front of the screen. "If you don't let me in," he says, "I will come in anyway and do the repair. I don't want to be out of a job because of you. Open the door, please."

Nile narrows his eyes and lets out a frustrated huff. The image fades to black. The screen retracts back into the doorframe and Jeshan readies himself. He places his hand over the holster strapped to his leg. He can hear movements within, then some beeping noises from the door's security keypad being decoded from the inside. Locks and bolts snap open, and a cloud of steam covers Jeshan's feet as the hydraulics begin to work. The sound is almost deafening.

As the doors open, Jeshan feels that Nile hasn't bought his story, so he clears himself from view, but only just in time.

A loud blast from a firearm surges through the opening. The sound of it is enough to make Jeshan's ears burst. The blast leaves a dark, melting hole in the adjacent wall. Jeshan unholsters his weapon. Another blast shatters the metal of the doorframe. Small, sharp fragments shoot into the back of Jeshan's shoulder, forcing a cry as he falls. A loud laugh comes from within the apartment. "Take that, you fuck."

Nile fires again.

Jeshan gets to his feet with his head swimming. He has underestimated this guy's fury, and the mistake has nearly cost him his life. He focuses, and his mind recognizes the sound and power of the firearm. A Plasma F-K80, a space police riot gun, a common grab on the black market after the rise in crime. He knows of the gun's faults; its charge can only last for four blasts before it needs to repower. Nile has already spent three. The recharge cycle takes ten seconds, more than enough time for Jeshan to make his move. "You need to do better than that!" Jeshan calls in, trying to ignore the pain in his shoulder and the ringing in his ears.

Nile fires.

A chiming bell sounds from the Plasma F-K80, signaling the beginning of its recharge cycle.

"Shit!" Nile yells. He shakes the weapon like it's malfunctioning.

Jeshan steps into the doorway and fires a round into Nile's left leg. The man screams and collapses to the floor. Jeshan walks over and kicks the Plasma out of his hands, then shakes the fuzziness from his head, and the ringing in his ears subsides.

"Wait a minute!" Nile cries holding up a hand. "W-we can talk about this."

Jeshan sinks his boot into Nile's throat. The target squirms in agony and begins to choke. Jeshan takes aim at his head, but he hears a noise. It's coming from a nearby room. He looks down at Nile fiercely. "Who was that? Who's in there?"

He reaches for Nile's riot gun and holds it at the ready. "Don't move an inch!" The wound in his own shoulder feels as if it's being prodded with hot spikes. Channeling his pain, he proceeds down the hall of Nile's apartment with his guns aimed at the far door. The poor lighting in the corridor flickers as he descends into its throat.

He presses the open button and tenses his stance as the inner gloom faces him. His eyes snap to the rapid movement of something scuttling for cover. Jeshan peers deeper into the gloom and sees what moved in the dark.

She is crouched behind an overturned armchair and crying into her hands. Jeshan sighs and rolls his eyes; he will get no richer this night. A girl. Not a year over twelve. "Where's my daddy?" she cries out of the shadows.

Jeshan lowers his guns and relaxes.

His shoulders slump. His thoughts are of Arial. He is bound to do the same for this one as he did for her. He must obey the blue of her eyes. The eyes of life and hope. He must save them, not kill them. Decroid's power supply will have to wait. He turns and walks back to Nile's side. The wounded man lifts himself up onto his elbows as Jeshan crouches.

Nile's eyes dart with bewilderment. "Sh-she's all I have! You can k-kill me, but pl-please, don't hurt her."

Jeshan looks at the steaming wound in Nile's leg. "Let's bandage you up," he says, looking into the lucky bastard's eyes. "You and your daughter have a shuttle to catch."

Jeshan escorts Nile and his daughter through the gates of the shuttle station and off into a personnel-only passage. The wound in his shoulder burdens him, but he does his best to conceal his discomfort. In the passage they meet with Alice.

"What's happening? Who is this?" Nile whimpers.

"This is Alice. She will get you to Earth. Do as she tells you," Jeshan says.

"Earth has nothing for us. What will we do?"

"If you stay here, you will die. Both of you. When you land on Earth, man up and get a job pushing a broom. If this little girl is what you are living for, then swallow your fucking pride. Got it?"

Nile nods.

Jeshan and Alice share a glance. "Get 'em outta here," he says.

Alice nods and allows them through the door. Jeshan can see Arial in the other room. When she notices him, she leaps up from her colouring pages and runs and hugs his leg. It has taken him a few times like this to understand how to return affection, and he is still struggling, more so now with a shoulder wound. He simply pats her back.

"You doin' all right, kiddo?"

"Ya-ha!" she begins and looks up. "Alice doesn't let me have candy after supper."

Jeshan and Alice look at each other, and she gives him a wink. "You make sure you listen to Alice, okay? She looks after you now."

"When can I see you again?" Arial asks.

"Don't know. I'll try not to make it too long this time."

Arial hugs his leg again and goes back to her colouring pages. Alice steps outside the doorway with Jeshan and closes the door behind her.

"What the fuck happened to you?" Alice asks.

"It's just a small wound. Nothing to worry about."

"It's Arial I'm worried about. Talks of you all of the time. How the fuck am I going to explain to her beautiful eyes that something has happened to you!"

"This wound was my fault. I'll be more careful."

Alice lets out a sigh and says, "Arial misses you."

"She hardly knows me."

"When a mother gives life to a child, then that would come first in forming a lifetime bond. However, saving a life comes in a pretty close second."

"I can't thank you enough for taking her in."

"I've always wanted kids, but I can't have them. Arial is a blessing."

"She looks happy."

"She could be happier."

Jeshan sighs. "I have business I need to take care of. I will try and stop by more often. I just don't know what she wants from me."

"You *have* been locked in the dark, haven't you? All she wants is for you to sit with her and read her a book, or watch her do her colouring pages."

"I'd love to do those things. But times are complicated right now. I am working hard to try and make them simpler."

Alice leans her arm back through the door and brings out a case that makes Jeshan's eyes widen with wonder. "Does your business involve using this? I can't do this again. I can get thrown into jail for stuff like this. This item looks expensive."

"You found one? Where?" Jeshan gasps.

"I snatched it off a freighter. Is it what you asked for? I wasn't sure of the model number."

"Don't worry, it's perfect," Jeshan says as he gives it a brief inspection. "Thank you, Alice. If all goes accordingly, you will both see me very soon."

For Jeshan, the device means that he can make his war.

The fuel gauge on Jeshan's cruiser is in the red, but he is able to get into his hangar. He sets his craft down, gets out awkwardly, and nurses his shoulder with every move. He grunts his way into the hanger's elevator and ascends to his floor. The unit Alice has stolen for him is heavy, nearly too heavy with his injury. He struggles to his apartment and swipes his card.

Decroid speaks before the doors are fully open. "Power?"

"I prefer the more pleasant greetings," Jeshan sighs. "You know, like good morning, good evening, nice to see you." He drops his card on the metal counter. "They were better to come home to."

Decroid watches his every movement, its lenses turning and adjusting in the dark and its processor ticking and scanning. Jeshan grunts and drops the heavy unit casing at his feet. He loosens the straps of his leg holster and falls on the couch. The wound in his shoulder complains as he examines it with tender fingers.

Decroid cocks its head. "Why . . . injured?"

"I got sloppy."

"No . . . kill?"

"No."

Jeshan rests his head back.

Decroid continues to dangle the outlet plug in front of him. "Power?"

Jeshan stares. "I have a surprise for you."

The machine cocks its head.

Jeshan stares at Decroid, and after a moment he stands up. He opens the casing at his feet and pulls out a large cable. He activates a switch on the portable power unit and takes Decroid's outlet plug from its metal digits. Decroid's processor ticks and spins in a rhythm that signifies excitement.

Connected.

"Engage," Jeshan utters.

Decroid's back straightens immediately as a program etched into its processor launches. Like blood flowing into a starved body, the electricity surges through Decroid's wiring. The hydraulics in its legs lift it upward so its eye level is above that of its master. Jeshan contemplates the two-inch guns that are mounted on Decroid's hips. The shield casing of the robot's chest is mapped with battle dents. Its metal hands open, extending steel digits; sharp, chrome pins protrude from each fingertip. All of them drip with a lethal toxin. In its day, the Droid was a fine battle unit, deployed along with one hundred others by the desperate authorities from Earth to aid in their war against the Baxter empire. A war that was not won.

A war that is not over.

"What is our objective?" Jeshan asks, and with a voice lower in tone, Decroid answers his master. "Myles Baxter . . . kill."

Jeshan grins.

"We will, my friend. It's time."

Jeshan gives himself a few days to heal. He has managed to steal several liters of fuel from some of the other crafts in the hanger, enough at least to transport himself and Decroid to their battleground. The time has also allowed him to study Baxter Plaza and the security that Myles has implemented. A barrier, along with a checkpoint, has been built a few yards from the building's entrance.

Jeshan has waited until nightfall to launch their attack, with Decroid leading the assault. He is equipped with his armored vest. He straps on an appropriate number of guns and daggers. Locking down the face guard to his helmet, which is equipped with night vision, he deploys Decroid. The checkpoint is reduced to rubble and fire within seconds, and Decroid marches through it, its two-inch guns thundering, turning any guard in range into a splatter of mangled and burning flesh. Its bullets have been designed to penetrate armored vehicles, so one can only imagine the devastation they cause a vessel made only of flesh and bone.

Jeshan leaps through the fire and fights alongside his Droid. The foyer of the plaza is greeted with an assault of Decroid's cannon fire. Within moments, they neutralize all of the Baxter guards there and ascend to the top floor. "Excellent, Decroid," gasps Jeshan through his mask.

Decroid is the first to exit the elevator. A shower of blaster fire sprays sparks off its metal frame and chest plate. There are more guards on the top floor. Jeshan releases dozens of gas grenades into the lightning of fire that forces Decroid to step backward. The Droid returns deafening rounds with its guns, but the onslaught of heavy fire confuses its aim.

The gas proves fruitful and allows Jeshan to shield himself behind his Droid and exterminate the remaining guards. As the gas clears, he can see that the hall is littered with a sea of bloodied bodies. Man and Droid make their way to the door of the penthouse. Decroid crushes bone and dead flesh with its heavy steps and reduces the door to rubble with one blast from its cannons.

Inside there are a dozen guards to deal with. Decroid focuses, homing in on targets on each of their heads within seconds, and deploys an instantaneous round of bullets, beheading them all. Jeshan and Decroid enter through pools of blood. Myles is in the centre of the room, a blaster held in a trembling hand.

Jeshan shoots it out of his grip, the blast melting three of Myles's fingers. Myles falls to the floor, yelling and gripping the bleeding and spurting stubs. Jeshan approaches with his Droid in tow. He takes off his mask and enjoys the look of terror on the fallen king.

"Uncle? You have to remember that we are family," Myles yells.

"Never stopped you."

"We ca-ca-can talk about this. I'll give yo-you anything!"

"You must have me confused with someone who gives a fuck."

Myles is silent.

Jeshan faces Decroid and examines the damage it sustained during their entrance into the plaza. There is some breakage to the left leg, but aside from that, it is impressively intact, considering the amount of fire it has taken.

"What do you want from me? Do you want me to confess that I–I had my father killed? Is that it? All right, then, I did it. Uncle! You hear me? I set the whole thing up."

"This is one impressive machine," Jeshan says, ignoring Myles. "Do you know what it is?"

Myles says nothing. He just stares, and Jeshan continues. "This was one of the battle Droids that was deployed many years ago to destroy your father's empire. They were well built, but underequipped, which is why they failed. I made some of my own additions to its equipment. Now, it is the Droid it should've been."

Jeshan rises and faces Myles again. "But there was one original tool I didn't remove from the machine. This will impress you."

He turns to Decroid and orders, "Decroid, initiate objective."

Decroid walks towards Myles. The crime boss screams, "Get that fucking thing away from me!"

"Baxter . . . kill!" Decroid says as it extends one of its arms towards the mobster.

Chrome pins protrude out of each of Decroid's fingers and stab into Myles's chest. Decroid retracts its arm and backward-steps to its master's side. Myles grabs at his chest, screaming and squirming.

"The government were naive to think they could ever get that close to your father. At least the tool will not go in vain."

"What the fuck is in me?" Myles mutters, feeling a substance hotter than boiling water enter his blood stream.

"The machine has injected you with a lethal toxin. It will destroy cells in some parts of you and regenerate some in others. The process is completely random. It is designed to bring the victim as much pain as possible. Goes to show how much the government despised your father and the crime wave, to invent something more inhumane than the crimes themselves. You must respect this, considering how much you like others to suffer."

The toxin is doing its work on Myles. The inner walls of his legs cave in as if they are deflating. A tooth from his lower jaw begins to grow unnaturally, surging up and through the roof of his mouth. The tooth continues to grow until it protrudes through his head like an ice pick. Myles is still alive up until the cells in his brain dissolve, one by agonizing one. Jeshan grins as Myles's head deflates like a sad melon. Hissing. Steaming. Melting.

"It is over," says Decroid. "Empire . . . destroyed."

"No, Decroid. Not destroyed."

Tick, spin. Tick spin.

"Overthrown," Jeshan continues.

He steps before his Droid and says, "We run things now."

"New . . . objective?"

"I have two people I want you to guard."

Tick, spin. Tick spin. "Sentinel . . . safeguard . . . protector."

"That's correct, Decroid."

"Your . . . directive?"

"To help Parhelion realize its destiny."

THE DOWNFALL

An Interview with
DAVID SCHEMBRI
by Paula Berinstein

David, why do you write horror?

It might seem strange to hear, but I ponder that question from time to time: Why *do* I write horror?

The answer is, to have a voice in a literary genre I've come to admire. No matter how small that voice may be in a realm of wonderful and larger entities, it's there. In print. Online. On someone's mobile reading device, being read, and I hope, being enjoyed and worthy of someone's time.

People are always surprised when they find out I write stories of a dark nature. Their expression is always the same, and they always ask the same question.

"Oh, you write? What do you write about?" they ask enthusiastically.

"I write horror stories," I say.

I then see, almost in slow motion, the drooping of their smiles, the raising of their eyebrows, and perhaps even a backward step!

I go on to explain that horror is an emotion, and my stories express that feeling in many environments. After that, they seem to relax to some degree. Some of them go on to ask me more; some change the subject.

In many ways, I am hardly what one would label a horror fanatic. I am not a big fan of horror films. Scary *literature* is my passion. My interest in the genre began when I was a teenager. I picked up a book of Richard Laymon's stories and read it. I promptly purchased another, and then another. The day I picked up a horror novel, far thicker than anything I'd read before, I felt excited at the prospect of reading a book that could spook me. Could literature do this?

It did, and it created an exhilarating feeling every time I read; thus my respect and admiration for horror literature blossomed. I eagerly consumed tales of the weird and the wonderful, the crazy and the bizarre, the dark and the terrible. I was immersed; I was hooked. And so my writing took shape during this foray into the lands of the horrific.

How long have you been writing horror, and has your approach changed over time?

I wrote my first tales during my secondary education, when I would write on a weekly basis in a compulsory journal. My teacher in literature at the time was fascinated as well as disturbed by my writings. He couldn't understand a well-behaved student who was pleasant and friendly, yet wrote tales of such a nature. He took me aside once and spoke to me about my horror journals and asked, "Why don't you try something different? Nonfiction? Document your week as a student?"

The next week's entry in my journal stated that I was bored and had no creative outlet. I also said that my horror journal was the only form of home study I really looked forward to, as I loved creating stories. My teacher read this and laughed, then told me I could continue my works. The following year he spoke to my parents at a parent/teacher interview and stated with confidence that their son was going to be a writer.

I wrote my first chapter story, *Zega*, at the age of ten. I used an old typewriter. I closeted myself in my bedroom and wrote my little heart out. I even left space on some of the pages for illustrations.

Zega was about a giant monster. It began with a meteor colliding with the earth, landing in the fields of a military outpost in desert America. This strange object was inspected in the military laboratory and ended up being an alien's egg. The egg hatched; the alien, Zega, emerged, and all hell broke loose. The galactic creature also grew to gigantic proportions before the end of the tale, and I paid quite a bit of attention to the commander of the outpost, who ended up being more of a villain than the monster. No one has ever read this story. Nor have I revealed the plot to anyone in such detail—only a few select people (two of them being my parents).

However, after I wrote *Zega*, I knew writing creepy things was something I enjoyed. I liked being allegorical and not didactic. I was about thirteen when my stories turned darker. At this immature age my stories were filled with bloodshed and influenced by late night horror movies. This was especially apparent in my *Journals of Horror*, which I wrote during secondary school.

The better the literature I read, the better my stories became. Horror was the underlying element, but story and characters were the drivers. My knowledge of literature was improving as I came to understand that even in horror, your characters need to evoke human interest and your narrative needs to be backed up by reasoning. The reading of great horror masters such as King, Laymon, and Barker kept me inspired, and my stories were becoming more expansive.

I wrote my first novel over ten years whilst taking train trips from design job to design job. The final book, *While the Day Sleeps*, was entirely hand written in a grouping of exercise books. I only have one copy and it is in a safe place—I think. Wait a minute—where is it?

My second novel remains incomplete because my interest turned to short story writing before I could finish it. I felt that if I could grasp the technique of writing shorter works, I would be better prepared to give my novels the time they deserved. This change in direction was sparked not only by joining the Australian Horror Writers Association, but also by taking a judgment seat in the 2006 Australian Shadows Awards. Now I was being exposed to some very strong local talent, all exercising profound skill in the art of speculative fiction. Authors such as Robert Hood, Stephen Dedman, Marty Young, Kaaron Warren, and David Conyers opened the floodgates to a world I was unaware of. I turned my sights to the speculative format, and I am so glad I did.

When I first started submitting short story work for publication in 2006, I wrote intuitively. I acted on story subjects and ideas immediately, and I would write until I was satisfied with the tale. I would then edit for quite some time before I was ready to submit it anywhere. This approach led to reasonable success with flash and micro fiction over the years.

My style and approach has changed quite a lot since then. I tend to take a deep breath before writing a short horror story nowadays. When I have a tale I wish to bring to life, research comes first, then character development, then the first draft. I find this to be a good system as every story I've approached in this manner has made it through the gate—gates I would never have dreamed of opening a few years ago.

When you start, do you see the characters the way they eventually emerge in your art work, or are there differences?

The art reflecting my characters starts where I initially see them in the literature. However, they become somewhat clearer after I've developed and written them. I never settle for second best. When I draw them, they must match my vision or I'll abandon the sketch. My art for *Parhelion: Rage of the Starborn* is a good example. Decroid, Jeshan, and

Baxter all transferred to the art fluently, as was the case with the art for *The Tuning of Hex*.

The work that demanded a little more attention when designing was the series for *Vow's Passage*. I had intended to illustrate two pieces for that story, but one composition did not transfer well enough from concept to final, so I extended the series to three.

If you could illustrate a famous horror story, what would you pick and why?

This is one hard question, my dear friend. I think I would have to go with H.P Lovecraft's "The Rats in the Walls." I feel that the dimension and vividness of his visions would be a great delight to design and illustrate, from the dark moments where you hear the sounds about the house—where mood and lighting could play an integral part—to the rich imagery leading towards the end, where the central characters bear witness to horrors piled upon horrors.

What's the horror story you haven't written yet, are afraid to write, and may or may not ever do?

No story has filled me with more trepidation than my first attempt at a short fiction tale. Regrettably, the very best I can do for you here is to discuss a piece that I began and didn't complete, as I have no unwritten tales in my head at present that I'm too anxious to write. The story in question marks the first time I'd begun to write a short tale since putting the brakes on my second novel.

I had written three drafts of it and it was given birth by a vivid dream. I didn't think too much of the subject matter at the time, nor did I fully grasp how brutal the tale was until a couple of years later. When I revisited the 7500+-word piece briefly after several anthology and magazine placements, I was taken aback. I believe this was because I'd recently become a father. Don't misinterpret me; the story contains no violence or mistreatment of minors, but as a young father raising a beautiful child, I just didn't feel an interest in pursuing a tale that focused purely on human ugliness and butchery. As with all stories I write, there was logic and even a moral, but *that* particular piece? The horror was too extreme for comfort.

Now that my family is growing and my handling of literature has matured, I might gain enough courage to tackle the twisted halls of that story again and approach it from the ground up.

The title was "Lockback and the Red Hawk."

THE GLIMPSE

Author and Artist

David is an Australian writer who lives in the mountains of Victoria with his lovely wife and two children. His stories have been receiving acceptances since 2006, and have appeared in a wide variety of publications. To note are: *Undead & Unbound, Eulogies II: Tales from the Cellar,* and *The Big Book of New Short Horror.* David's horror/fantasy poetics have also been published by Rainfall Books and the Hippocampus Press magazine, *Spectral Realms.*

David also is a published artist and runs a design studio.